Spurs for José

Wanda Snow Porter

In the memory of
Charles Porter

The author wishes to extend her gratitude to John Porter,
Barbara Watson, Michael O'Brien, and Dr. Clifford E. Trafzer
for their expert advice and help.

Spurs for José

Chapter One
~*The Rodeo* ~

Salty sweat burned José's eyes. He pulled off his rumpled, wide-brimmed hat and wiped his sweaty brow. Waiting for the next calf to brand, he adjusted the eagle feather stuck in his hatband and watched hawks flying above the golden hills bordering the eastern edge of Rancho Grande's thirty-eight-thousand acres. His gaze followed their flight west toward the brush-covered dunes that protected the valley from chilly ocean winds.

Bellows of cattle echoed in the peaceful valley. It was the fall of 1846, late in the year for a rodeo. However, this year on the Alta California rancho, hundreds of calves were born during the summer months, too many to wait for next spring's branding.

A vaquero threw his loop, lassoed a calf's heels, and stretched it on the ground, ready for the rancho's brand.

José brushed back a strand of dark hair, shoved the hat deep on his head, and then carefully picked up the red-hot branding iron.

Commotion was all around him as he darted between horses and avoided the running and bucking calves fighting the lasso. The hot iron sizzled against the calf's furry hip. The stink of burning hair rose to his nostrils, a smell he knew well.

He watched for the angry mother cow that could charge if her calf was threatened. He finished branding and removed the tight lasso from around the calf's hooves.

"José, come here," Diego shouted over the bawling cattle.

José cautiously ran out of the ring of cows, horses, and men to where his papa sat astride a palomino horse guarding the circle's boundary. He stood next to his papa's horse and gazed up, squinting against the sun's glare.

Diego Rodriquez, half Chumash Indian, was born at Mission San Luis Obispo de Tolosa and was given his father's Spanish name when baptized by the padre. A fine horseman, he trained the rancho's horses.

José admired his papa's skill. It took courage to ride the twisting, bucking broncos. Someday, like his brothers, he would be expected to help tame the wild horses. He worried when that day came, perhaps he would not be brave enough to ride the mustangs.

Suddenly, Diego spun the palomino to chase a lanky calf trying to escape the huddled herd. He twirled his lasso twice, threw his reata quickly, caught the calf, and dragged it back into the herd.

Returning to his son, Diego said, "Go to the rancho, and tell Tomas we need more wood for the branding fire."

"*Sí*, Papa." José jumped on his black horse and galloped the mile to the ranchero's *casa*. Built on the edge of a mesa, it overlooked the grassy valley that spread for miles along a broad creek.

Near the grand *casa* stood a barn, a work shed for the blacksmith, and small adobes for the vaqueros. He dismounted and peered inside the barn, looking for Tomas and found him cleaning and repairing harness. He had been at the rancho as long as José could remember. His face, dark and wrinkled, was shriveled like dried leather from the many years spent in the sun driving the *carreta*, hauling hides and trade goods back and forth from the ships that landed at the cove.

"Tomas, we need more wood for the branding fire."

The old man cocked his head like a rooster and looked up from his work, surprised. He hadn't heard José come into the barn.

"What? What do you want?" Tomas peered at José with watery gray eyes. "Is that you, José?"

"*Sí*, I was sent to get more wood for the branding fire."

Tomas stood slowly, stretching his back with both hands grasping his skinny waist. "More wood? I'm not young anymore and need help loading it. Help me with the oxen."

He handed José a rope, and they went to the back of the barn where the oxen were tied. Leading an ox, Tomas pointed at the other ox of the team for him to lead.

With fingers creased black from the tallow he used to soften leather, Tomas secured the oxen to the *carreta*. "Come, let's load the wood."

Behind the barn, oak wood was gathered and stacked for fires used for cooking, making candles and soap, or heating tallow. Often, a smoke wrapped like a blanket around the barn's thick adobe walls. Tomas and José stacked wood inside the *carreta* and began the slow trek to the rodeo. With no road, they followed cow paths and deer trails, trusting the animals knew the easiest way to travel. The trail was rough. Squirrel holes with mounds of black dirt riddled the path.

While Tomas drove the oxen, José's horse plodded beside the rickety *carreta*. Like José's papa, Tomas was born at the mission. "Tell me about when you were young," José said. He liked hearing what it had been like living at the mission before the Indians worked on the ranchos.

Tomas laughed. "I didn't think anyone wanted to hear those old stories anymore. *Sí*, I was a vaquero once. It was long ago. Then the mission had thousands of cattle. They needed vaqueros, so the padres taught me how to ride and rope."

José smiled. He had heard this story many times.

The old man shook his head. "Until Mexico took the mission's land, it was the only home I knew. Now, instead of the padres, the ranchero owns the land and trades with the captains."

Tomas's stories made the slow ride seem shorter. Soon they arrived at the rodeo, and sunburned, barefoot boys jumped into the *carreta* while it crept along.

"Get down!" Tomas yelled. "Since you have so much energy, you can help unload this wood."

Tomas halted the oxen just outside the circle of cattle. José helped the other boys toss the wood in a pile, laughing and teasing as they worked.

Pedro, the blacksmith's son, had been watching the rodeo, but now started throwing dirt at the boys.

"Pedro, stop! Wild cattle aren't used to loud children running and yelling." Old Tomas had little patience when work was to be done.

José filled his arms with wood, carried it to the branding fire, and threw chunks of dry oak onto the hot coals. As he tramped back to the outskirts of the circle, a wild-eyed cow dashed past the vaqueros.

"Watch out!" José leaped in front of the cow, waving his arms, trying to turn her back toward the herd.

But he couldn't.

The cow wagged her head from side to side. Slinging slobber and snot, she ran straight at the laughing boys. She lowered her head, knocked Pedro down, and shoving with her horns, rolled him over and over.

Two vaqueros raced over and lassoed the cow's front feet and pulled their reatas tight, throwing her to the ground. She bellowed, hanging her tongue out of her mouth.

José ran to Pedro and rolled him over. He was unconscious, his face ashen.

"Pedro. Pedro," José shouted. "Are you all right? Can you hear me?"

José's papa was quickly by his side. Lifting Pedro, he placed him in the *carreta*. "Take him to the rancho, Tomas. And José, ride ahead and let Pedro's papa know what happened. Hurry!"

Chapter Two
~Roping the Grizzly Bear~

José swung into his saddle and rushed to the rancho. Dodging squirrel holes, he galloped his horse, sliding to a stop in front of the blacksmith's shed.

"Señor Eduardo! Señor Eduardo!"

Eduardo hurried outside. "Why all this yelling? What's wrong?"

"Pedro's hurt. At the rodeo, a loco cow charged and knocked him out. Tomas is bringing him in the carreta."

Usually soft-spoken, Señor Eduardo said in a loud voice, "Pedro's hurt? Where is he? I'll saddle a horse."

"Take mine," José offered and quickly dismounted. Eduardo leaped on the horse and galloped toward the rodeo.

José's hands still trembled from all the excitement. He took a deep breath to steady his galloping heartbeat and went inside the blacksmith's shed to wait for Tomas and Pedro.

It was dim inside, lit by hot coals used by the blacksmith to heat cold iron to make many things needed on the rancho. The shop fascinated José. He liked to watch Señor Eduardo's muscular arms bang his hammer against hot iron, beating and twisting it into interesting and useable shapes.

Along the roof's edge, rusty hinges, iron bits, and sharp-pointed spurs hung on nails. Shiny silver spurs lay on the blacksmith's workbench.

José fingered the finely engraved metal and noticed the rancho's brand in the design. These spurs belonged to the ranchero. José wished to own a pair like them and imagined silver spurs on the heels of his boots.

Señor Eduardo's angry voice awakened him from his daydream. "Pedro, you're too old to be playing. If you had been working, you wouldn't have gotten hurt!"

José hurried out of the shop. "Are you all right, Pedro?"

"I'm a little dizzy, and my head hurts, but I think I am all right. I cannot remember what happened. I woke up when the *carretta* hit a big squirrel hole. It was such a rough ride I decided to walk. Until Papa came with a horse."

"An angry cow charged and knocked you down," José said. "Lucky for you, the vaqueros lassoed her. Otherwise, you'd be dead. You were lucky today. Very lucky."

"And very foolish," Tomas said as he entered the yard driving the team of oxen. "Luck won't save a fool. Those cows can kill you." He drove the slow team into the barn.

"*Sí*, Pedro," his papa said. "You were foolish. The cows protect their calves from anything that threatens them. Remember that!"

Señor Eduardo offered José the reins. "*Gracias,* for the use of your horse."

"I better get back to the rodeo. They'll wonder what happened."

José returned to the rodeo and told his papa about Pedro. Diego turned the palomino to face his son. "I'm glad he is fine. You were brave, trying to protect him. I have been thinking. At least twelve summers have passed since you were born. It is time for you to ride the young colts."

He didn't feel ready or brave. It had happened so fast. He had helped Pedro without thinking. Perhaps, if he had thought, he wouldn't have jumped in front of that crazy cow.

Diego was the rancho's horse trainer, one of the most important jobs on the rancho. José's pride was mingled with fear. He wanted to tame wild horses and learn all his papa's horse-training secrets. He wanted to be brave and fearless as his bronco-busting papa and make him proud José was his son.

When small and unable to handle the reins, José rode behind his papa. Then, when older, he was given a well trained horse to ride. For fun, he often joined the other children when they tried to ride the bucking calves the vaqueros had roped.

Except, wild colts were not as easy to ride as the little calves. Wild horses bucked and twirled. One had crippled Tomas. And last year, José's brother was badly injured training a fresh young horse. No, riding wild colts was not easy.

"Now, you are old enough," Diego continued, turning his gaze back on the cattle. "A vaquero must listen to the horse's snorts and whinnies, learn to understand his language, and become part horse."

He patted the palomino's neck. "You must understand the cow. She is tricky, and you must outthink her. We are on horseback from sunrise until darkness. It is the vaquero's way of life."

José's heartbeat thumped in his ears. He tried to swallow the tightness in his throat. "Next spring?"

"Next spring."

Before José could ask any more questions, his papa spurred his palomino out of the way of a bucking horse upset by a reata trapped under its tail. All the vaqueros stopped to watch. Finally, the frightened horse was circled into a halt, and everyone went back to work.

One of the young vaqueros galloped over to Jose. "Is Pedro dead?"

"No, but tomorrow he will ache from head to foot."

The vaquero laughed. "I hope he can dance at the fiesta. He'll be angry if anyone else dances with Carmelita."

"*Sí*, the fiesta. Pedro would dance to Carmelita's tune even if his legs were tied together, and he had to hop to the music." José laughed but was haunted with worry about riding the wild colts.

The next morning, he went to the barn to watch Tomas braid a reata. Even though he was strict, José enjoyed helping the old man braid strings of rawhide into useful and beautiful things.

"Take it apart and do it again. Your braid isn't tight enough," Tomas would say. Or, "Take it apart and do it again. The rows aren't straight enough."

Used to rope cattle, a reata had to be strong and tightly braided. The vaqueros' lives depended on them. José had to braid and braid over and over again under Tomas's watchful eyes.

"I heard your papa has decided you should start riding the wild ones," old Tomas said when José entered the barn. "I'll make new chaps for you, a pair of your own, not your brothers' old castoffs. You have grown tall this summer."

Tomas squinted, measuring José with his eyes. "I'll see if I have enough leather to fit your long legs."

"José, are you here?" Diego peered inside the barn and wasn't surprised to find his son helping the old man. "A grizzly bear has been seen in a canyon up the valley. We're riding out to rope him for the fiesta. Today you will ride with us."

"A grizzly?" A knot twisted in José's chest.

Learning to rope, he had practiced catching bushes, tree limbs, and anything that walked, including his sisters. When good enough with the reata, José began roping calves at the rodeo.

But roping a grizzly wasn't like roping calves. No, the great bear was fearless and fierce. Grizzlies had killed and injured many vaqueros.

"You will ride Santo. He has seen grizzlies before. Come, we must start before it's too hot." Diego walked out the door, not looking back, expecting his son to follow.

Jose stared at the empty doorway. He should go, but his boots seemed rooted to the floor.

Tomas reached out, turned José to face him, and gazed into his wide, brown eyes. "The mighty bear should be feared. Be careful. Only a fool would not fear him. Fear teaches respect. Never let your horse turn away from the big bear. Keep Santo straight with your spurs so he will not spin or panic."

He patted José's shoulder. "Your papa trained Santo to be brave and never refuse. You are ready, or your papa would never ask you to ride with him. Now go."

Tomas rubbed his stiff leg, then turned and limped into the twilight of the musty barn.

His papa and brothers were saddling their horses when José walked up. Santo was tied to a fence post, not yet brushed. He started brushing the stallion's fine golden coat. The horse watched him out of the corner of his eye, not sure who this young boy was, not sure if he liked the touch of this stranger's hand.

José quietly talked as he readied the horse for the saddle. By the time the saddle was cinched, the stallion had decided to accept him, letting out a soft snort when the cinch had tightened around his belly.

"Hurry up," his brother said.

José quickly slipped on his rusty spurs and wrapped his chaps around his thighs. He pulled the headstall over Santo's ears, and the horse eagerly slurped the copper roller of the spade bit, making a soothing, clicking sound.

He pulled himself into the saddle and followed, listening to his brothers joke and tease while riding the trail leading north toward the canyon. It seemed like any other day. Except José knew differently.

Entering the canyon, the men stopped joking. They quietly followed a cow path, watching the ground for tracks. The wide mouth of the canyon narrowed, and the sides grew steep as they rode deeper into the arroyo.

Time seemed strangely still.

"Look, there," Diego whispered, pointing at the ground.

In the soft dirt, giant bear tracks led farther into the canyon. Now, everyone became tense and ready. They shook out their reatas, prepared in case the grizzly bear rushed them from the bushes.

José did too, gulping for air as his heart raced. He stiffened his shoulders, hoping the others wouldn't notice his shaky hands. He tried to sit steady in the saddle and not let Santo feel his fear but knew the horse probably wasn't fooled.

The vaqueros slowed their horses, listening for sounds of the bear's presence. A soft crackle alerted them that something big might be in the bushes.

With amazing speed, a grizzly rushed out, and the ten-foot giant stood on his hind legs ready to attack.

Santo, showing his warhorse bloodlines, raised his flowing white tail, held it high and trumpeted a loud, challenging snort.

José was surprised by Santo's noisy outburst but kept his spurs near the stallion's sides.

"Stay back, José, until I tell you to come!" Diego yelled.

His brothers quickly threw loops over the bear's giant head, pulling in opposite directions.

The roaring bear's terrible teeth and claws lashed out at the reatas and tried to pull the riders toward him into slashing paws.

Diego threw his lasso, caught the bear's hind legs, and stretched him on the ground to stop him from biting the reatas to shreds. The huge bear continued to fight, roar, and roll in the dirt, his forepaws struggling to free himself.

"Now, José! Now! Catch his paws!"

José spurred Santo closer to the beast, twirling his lasso overhead. The angry bear roared and raised dust as he twisted and struggled, making it difficult for him to be sure when to throw his loop.

"Now! Hurry!" his papa yelled again, causing José to rush and throw his loop at the fearful paws, missing. His reata glanced against the grizzly's head, becoming entangled as the bear still lashed out.

Next to José, his brother hurriedly threw a loop and caught the huge paws. With reatas stretched tightly, his brothers continued to pull in different directions to keep the grizzly off balance. Then they wrapped a reata around the bear to secure him on the ground.

Frantic, the grizzly fought to regain his feet. Finally, he lay quietly.

Diego dismounted. "José get off your horse. Come here. Bring your lasso."

He coiled his forty-foot reata and then dismounted Santo, who fearlessly stood while José walked carefully to his papa.

Diego pointed at the great-clawed feet. "Tie his forepaws tight."

Awed by the size of the grizzly, José cautiously wrapped the lasso around and around the dangerous paws.

"Now, tie his jaws shut."

Following his papa's instructions, he tightly bound the fierce nose and sharp teeth. The bear panted. José smelled its hot, wet breath.

When the grizzly's paws and jaws were securely bound, the vaqueros loosened their lassos from the bear's neck, allowing it to breathe easier.

José's brother unrolled a bull hide, and they managed to drag and roll the beast onto it.

Mounting his horse, Diego said, "By the time we drag the bear back to the rancho on this hide, he will truly hate bulls."

Chapter Three
~ *The Fiesta*~

The hides and tallow were prepared for transport to the ships, and the harvest finished. It was time to give thanks and celebrate. José could hardly wait for the fiesta to begin. It was an exciting time on the rancho. The vaqueros played guitars and violins and danced with their wives. The women showed off new babies and new dresses.

Outside, a fire heated the *horno,* and huge chunks of beef were being barbequed over slow-burning coals. Women were preparing tamales, tortillas, and *frijoles* spiced with garlic and chilies. The delicious smell surrounded the ranchero's adobe *casa.* José's mouth watered.

Besides the grizzly he and his papa had captured, vaqueros had also lassoed a fierce bull and dragged him to the rancho. A fight between the two beasts would be the fiesta's entertainment. An event unequaled in ferocity, much gambling would take place on the outcome. Which great beast would be faster and tougher? Which great beast would win?

José went to the barn to tell Tomas about his adventure with the grizzly. "Tomas, did you see the grizzly we caught? Santo was brave. He challenged the bear." He didn't mention he wasn't as brave as the palomino stallion when the huge bear had rushed out of the bushes.

"Santo is bred to be brave enough to challenge a grizzly bear. The bull they captured is also brave and ferocious. He will be a fine rival for the old bear." Tomas laid aside the strings of rawhide he was braiding. "It will be a great battle. I am not sure on which one I will place my wager. They will fight to the finish. Neither will surrender."

In the yard, hens clucked and scattered as vaqueros from the neighboring rancho galloped past the barn door. Tomas walked to the door and yelled after them, "You crazy men, slow down! Children are playing in the yard."

Due to the long distances between the ranchos, neighbors seldom visited. They had been invited to join the feasting and the dancing. José went outside to see who had ridden over to join the fun.

"Uncle Miguel." He laughed as his uncle stepped down from his horse and hugged him. His uncle worked on a rancho a day's ride away, and they rarely saw him. Miguel liked to tease and joke with his nephew. José was happy to see him.

"You have grown as tall as your brothers since I saw you last summer," Miguel said. "I hear you rode with your papa to rope the grizzly."

It always amazed José how quickly people knew what was happening at the neighboring ranchos. Words traveled as fast as a man could ride across the grassy pastureland.

"*Sí*, Uncle, I helped capture him. I tied his great jaws. I've never been so close to a grizzly while he was still alive. I could feel his breath on my face."

"Do you think a bull will be a match for him?" his uncle asked, which surprised José. He had never been asked for his opinion before.

He frowned, remembering his fear of the powerful grizzly. "He is fierce. Tomas thinks the bull will be a good match, but I think the grizzly will win."

José's papa rode up while they were talking. Seeing his brother, he dismounted.

"Miguel, how long has it been? Did you come to watch the fight? What have you to wager, maybe a new hackamore? José will be breaking colts this spring. He needs a hackamore to start the wild ones. Maybe you'd wager the one your colt is wearing?"

"I'll decide after I see the bear and bull." Miguel mounted his horse. "Let's ride down to the corral. What will you wager? I need a new reata. I like yours. It will be a bet, eh?"

The two brothers rode down the steep hillside to the corral where the fight would be held. Tomas and José followed on foot. He waited while old Tomas hobbled slowly along.

In the corral, the grizzly was chained to a tree. The huge bear's hind leg was cautiously being tied to the bull's forefoot so they could not retreat from the fight. Diego and Miguel joined other vaqueros who had surrounded the enclosure with reatas ready, just in case the bull or bear did manage to escape.

Tomas and José pushed their way to the front of the gathering crowd. "Look at the size of that grizzly. No matter how brave the bull, I think the bear will win."

"He's even bigger when you are close to him," José said. "Those paws are the size of watermelons. When I tied them together, it took many wraps to secure those giant paws. The bull will have little chance to defeat him."

The excited crowd placed many bets, mostly on the grizzly. The two gigantic beasts were released from the tree. At first, the two animals tried to escape, running in opposite directions until the lasso holding them together tightened.

Then the bear turned and roared in anger, looking for what had pulled against him. The great bull also twisted around to face what had stopped him. Then he charged the mighty bear, lowering his head to use his long horns against his enemy. The grizzly saw the bull charging and took his stance, rising on his hind feet, ready to lash out.

When the two powerful creatures met, a cloud of dust swirled and billowed upward as they stomped the ground in battle. The crowd cheered. Through the hazy dust, José could see the savage battle, but Tomas's old eyes could not.

"What is happening?" Tomas asked and leaned closer to hear José.

"The grizzly struck the bull on his poll between the horns," José yelled over the cheering crowd. "Now the bull plunges a horn into the grizzly's belly. The bear is hurt but grasps the bull's horns and is clawing the hide off his neck. The grizzly's teeth have clamped onto the bull's nose, trying to throw him to the ground." He shook his head. "Both are wounded. Only rage is driving them to continue the fight. I don't think either will survive."

"I wish I could see so great a fight, such power, such bravery." Tomas looked down, listening to roars and snorts of the beasts as they twisted and turned in a death dance. "When your life is threatened, it is good to be brave. We must fight to survive, no matter what. Life is a great struggle. Remember, José, these creatures and how they battle. They teach us a lesson, to be fierce and never surrender. In surrender, we are defeated."

He grasped the old man's arm. "I wish you could see them. The bull is falling. The grizzly is trying to stand, but he, too, is falling."

As the dust settled, Jose felt sad when he saw the two huge animals, both injured beyond life, lying in a heap together. "Oh, Tomas, they are dying. Neither has won."

"No one loses their bet when both animals die." Tomas wiped the dust from his eyes with his shirtsleeve. "What great creatures. Their bravery honors both. This fight will be retold many times. When they are skinned, their hides will have magic powers." Tomas nodded. "Great power. I will make your chaps out of that brave bull's hide. I will ask your papa to claim it for you."

They elbowed their way through the crowd to where Diego and Miguel sat horseback. Tomas stared up at Diego. "José needs new chaps. I want to make them from the hide of that great bull. Make sure I get it. He is entitled to it. He helped capture the grizzly."

"He is," Diego agreed. "The bull hide will be his. It will bring him good luck to have chaps made from the brave bull's hide."

José knew that animals provided food for the rancho, and without death, there was no life. Even so, he felt sorry the bull had died. Yet something good would come from his death. From his hide, the bull's courageous spirit would pass into the chaps. When José wore them, they would give him courage and bring him luck. Then he would no longer fear to ride the young horses.

Diego threw his lasso around the dead bull's horns. "Miguel, come help me drag this bull to where the strippers can take his hide for José."

Miguel rode over and also threw a loop around the bull's long horns, and together the brothers dragged the heavy animal far away from the ranchero's *casa*. Other vaqueros secured their lassos around the bear, dragging him away to strip off his hide and claws.

That evening, José sat around a campfire outside his family's small adobe *casa* listening to his papa and uncle talk about all that had happened that day. Besides the fight, they also discussed a new government.

"It hasn't been so long ago that Mexico claimed the territory. Is Alta California going to change governments again?" Diego asked.

"Many think so," Miguel said. "I heard the United States raised its flag over Monterey, and an American named Fremont has an army that's marching from the north to Los Angeles. I think I will join this Fremont's army. He is paying vaqueros twenty-five dollars a month to make sure his army is fed. I've heard he is even paying Indians to join as scouts."

Uncle Miguel's eyes sparkled in the firelight. "Some are joining because they are angry. Others have a grudge against Mexico, but most just want the money."

"Twenty-five dollars," Diego said. "Going where? For how long? You have a wife and children. You cannot leave for months."

José's papa frowned. "No, Miguel. We are vaqueros, not soldiers. On horseback, no man looks down on us. We have no equal, no grudges, no enemies. Our life is here, on the rancho."

Miguel shook his head. "It doesn't sound hard, roping, and slaughtering cattle. We do it every day. With twenty-five dollars, I could buy many beautiful things."

Miguel rubbed his hands together. "You're wise, Diego, but we vaqueros barely make a living. A little food to feed our families and the clothing we need. Not much more. We *have* to work for the rancho. Where else can we go? We own nothing. Not even the horses we ride. Nothing."

"Will the United States treat us better than Mexico?" Diego asked. "Does it matter to us if Mexico or the United States rule Alta California? What if the United States loses this war?" He shrugged. "Then what? Can you go back to your rancho and work? Huh? With no job, how will your family eat? Our home and families are worth more than twenty-five dollars."

Miguel laughed. "The ranchero I work for is a Yankee. He came here and became a Mexican. I don't think he would mind if the United States claims Alta California. No, maybe he wouldn't mind at all." Both men stared into the fire, deep in thought.

José had never heard of Fremont. A war sounded exciting. He had lived on the rancho all his life. It was the same every year.

Life on the rancho followed the seasons. In the spring, calves were born, and crops planted. Summers were spent riding and roping, preparing tallow and hides for the big ships. In the fall, they prepared for winter when days were short and cold.

Nothing changed much unless the padre baptized a new baby or married a young couple. Then there was a fiesta and neighbors visited and danced and gambled.

Maybe an argument would start with vaqueros from neighboring ranchos, but by morning it was forgotten.

He wanted to go with Uncle Miguel, join the vaqueros marching with Fremont and earn twenty-five dollars. But he knew his papa would never permit him to go. Gazing into the burning coals, he thought of all the things the ranchero bought with his hides and tallow from the trade ships that came to the coast. He admired the ranchero's beautiful things. If he earned twenty-five dollars, then he could buy a pair of fancy spurs as the ranchero wore. Wearing silver spurs would double his luck when he rode the wild colts.

Pedro sat beside José, opening his palms toward the fire to warm his cold hands. "I hear Tomas is making you chaps from the bull's hide. He says the bull hide is lucky, but it is unlucky. The bull fell first, so he didn't win. No, I wouldn't want chaps made out of the hide of the loser. Those chaps will be cursed." Pedro glared his dark eyes at José.

He glared back at Pedro. "The bull was brave, and his hide will have magic power. Tomas said the chaps *would* be lucky."

"What would Tomas know about luck? Look at him. He is crippled. How do you think he got that way?

He was cursed. That's how, cursed and unlucky." Pedro stood and spat in the fire.

José stood too, clenching his fists. "Nobody asked you."

Pedro pushed his face into José's. Even though he was older, they were the same height. He grabbed José's hair and jerked back his head.

Punching Pedro's jaw with his fist, José knocked him backward onto the ground. Then he jumped on top of him, and they wrestled in the dirt.

"What is going on?" José's papa asked as he and Uncle Miguel pulled the two boys apart, lifting them to their feet. "You two settle down. You need to work harder if you have the energy to waste on fighting. Get more wood for the fire. Right now, go!"

The boys glared at each other as they dusted themselves off and went together to collect wood. They didn't speak as they carried armloads of wood back to where the men sat warming themselves. José was angry. Pedro had put doubt in his mind. Was the bull hide really cursed?

Chapter Four
~ *The Curse* ~

The next morning, José went to find Tomas. Entering the barn, he heard loud snores. Tiptoeing to the back of the barn, he found him wrapped in a serape sleeping next to the oxen. He looked small lying curled in a ball with his hands pillowing his cheek, clasped together as if in prayer.

As José turned to leave, Tomas called out, "Who's there?"

"It's me. I didn't know you were sleeping."

The old man stretched his arms overhead and yawned. "*Buenos días,* José. I am surprised you are up so early." Tomas staggered to his feet, using the wall to help gain his footing. "It is cold. Let's go out and sit by the fire."

José followed as Tomas wrapped the serape around his bony shoulders and limped outside. In the yard, muffled snores came from mounds of blankets covering men who had huddled near last night's fire.

"The fire is almost out." Tomas pointed toward a pile of wood stacked a few feet away. "Throw some wood on the coals."

He did so and then sat close to the fire on a crude log bench next to Tomas. Still upset from the night before, he silently watched as the dry logs popped and flared into hot flames.

Finally, Tomas said, "I heard you were in a fight last night."

After a long silence, José answered, "*Sí.*"

"I heard you fought with the blacksmith's son, Pedro."

"*Sí.*"

Tomas squinted to see José more clearly. "Well? What happened? Why were you fighting?"

"He said the bull was not brave, that he fell first, so chaps made from his hide will not be lucky."

"A stupid thing Pedro said made you mad enough to fight? The bull was *very* brave, and the chaps *will be* lucky. Pedro is wrong. Why do you care what he says?" Tomas looked at his hands and waited for an answer.

José stared into the fire. He'd rather bite his tongue than tell all the bad things Pedro had said but knew Tomas would keep asking until he learned the whole truth. "Pedro said you were cursed. That is why your leg was hurt. Because of a curse." He raised his head and peered at Tomas. "It isn't true, is it?"

"Are they still telling that story? What else did Pedro say? How much did he tell you?"

José widened his eyes. "Only that you were cursed and that is how your leg got hurt. A curse."

"*Sí*, it was a curse." Tomas clasped his wrinkled hands on his knees. "It is a sad story. It happened long ago when I was a young man, not much older than you. You wouldn't want to hear it."

"I want to hear. What happened?"

"Well, let me see." Tomas smacked his lips and stared into the fire. "It was a long time ago. I don't remember so good anymore, but I'll never forget Juanita. She was very beautiful and very wicked. She loved me and wanted to marry me, but I loved another. So, she cursed me."

"Juanita brought you bad luck?" José nodded. "Mama says there is nothing worse than a jealous woman."

Tomas shivered and pulled his serape tightly around his shoulders. "It *was* bad luck to be loved by Juanita. One fiesta, she put something in my drink. When I fell asleep, she stole the charm stone my mama gave me for protection and used it to put a curse on me. It was a small stone, shaped like a horse, carved by my papa. I always carried it."

Tomas stood and poked a stick at the burning coals, then again sat next to José.

After a minute of silence, José asked, "Then what happened?"

"My horse reared and fell backward on top of me. I was broken. Later, after I was hurt and unable to walk, she came crying to me and confessed she had crushed my charm stone with a hammer and ground the pieces under her feet. She was sorry and broke the curse, but by then it was too late."

The old man slowly shook his head and looked up from the fire. "She never married. No man trusted her. They all feared her magic. Years later, she was taken by a shark while wading in the ocean waves. Two lives changed forever. It is a sad story, but even so, the chaps made from that brave bull's hide *will be* lucky."

José clenched his fists. "Pedro is a liar."

"He is full of envy," Tomas said. "He is unhappy because you will have the honor of wearing those chaps. He wishes he were a vaquero. But he will always be a blacksmith, like his papa. Like you will always be a vaquero, like your papa. Don't listen to him."

Tomas stood and limped over to a big tub. "I better make sure the bull hide is still soaking. Pedro might have stolen it." Tomas leaned over and peered in. "No, it is still here soaking. We better move this tub into the barn. Come, help me pour out the water and take it inside."

Tomas's limp reminded José of how dangerous it was to ride the wild colts. A trace of fear crept into his heart. He needed the chaps to be lucky. He needed luck's protection when he rode the bucking colts. Then he could be brave. Pedro *had* to be wrong.

José helped drain the water out of the tub and carried it into the barn, setting it down where Tomas pointed. "Go get more water to fill this tub up again," Tomas said, and sent José to the creek.

Chapter Five
~ Captain Truckee ~

Days were growing colder. The sun set earlier and earlier each day. It was time to get ready for *La Noche Buena*. Preparing for the Christmas feast, women were soaking olives to get rid of their bitterness, and pumpkins and watermelons were candied. José could hardly wait to eat this sweet treat.

During these wintry days, the cattle roamed the hills looking for sprigs of new grass. Vaqueros had time to repair their riding gear needed for the spring rodeo. José followed his papa to the blacksmith shed, hoping Pedro wouldn't be there.

Outside the workshop, he heard the blacksmith's heavy hammer clanging against metal. It beat in a rhythm, one-and-two and one-and-two. Two hard beats, with a lighter, softer beat in between gave the blacksmith's strong arm a rest while he pounded the iron into a shape he wanted.

"*Buenos días*, Eduardo," Diego greeted the blacksmith as they entered his workshop. When the man turned, it was Pedro.

The two boys stared at each other. Their fight made José feel awkward.

"*Hola*, Señor Diego. What do you need?"

"I came for my spurs. Are they finished?"

Pedro laid his hammer aside. Water spat and sputtered as he dunked the red-hot iron into a bucket. "*Sí, Señor*. I will get them."

"Where is your papa today?" Diego asked.

"Rancho Gaviota. Their blacksmith got married and moved. I am in charge until Papa returns." Pedro handed Diego his dangerous-looking spurs with their sharp-pointed rowels.

While Diego inspected his spurs, José glanced at a bit laying on the workbench. Pedro noticed him gazing at his work and said, "Do you like the bit I am making, Señor Diego? The ranchero wants a new bit for Santo. Santo deserves a fine bit. It will be beautiful. The bit shanks will be inlaid with silver."

"Santo should have only the finest bit in his mouth," Diego said. "Make sure the balance is right. His mouth is sensitive. If you make a bit as well as your papa, it will be a superb one." Diego held the bit in the palm of his hand to feel its weight and balance. "It feels right. What do you think, José?"

José's papa handed him the bit to feel the weight and balance of the hard, cold iron. He fingered the mouthpiece, checking for rough edges that could tear a horse's soft tongue. Though still angry, he did admire Pedro's skill. "It feels smooth. I would like to see it when it's finished." He tried to keep the anger from his voice and not glare when he handed Pedro the bit.

Pedro smiled, proud of the skill he had learned from his papa, who was considered the best blacksmith around. Vaqueros from other ranchos wanted Eduardo to make bits and spurs for them, and now his son's skill would earn their respect, too.

Diego picked up his spurs and inspected them closely. "You have done a good job." The spur rowel clanked as he twirled it with his finger. "Will you make a pair for José? His feet have grown. He needs man-sized spurs."

Pedro peered at José's feet, smirked and winked. "I will be glad to make a pair of spurs to fit those boots. Try on your papa's spurs to see if they fit."

The other boy's smug expression irritated José. He wore his older brother's too-big, hand-me-down boots with worn-out, curled toes. His papa said they would give his feet room to grow.

José's face grew hot as he squatted on one knee to place the spur on the heel of his boot. "*Sí,* this one fits." He frowned and handed the spur back to his papa.

"I'll start working on your spurs tomorrow and make them just the right size for those boots," Pedro said.

As José and Diego left the blacksmith's shop, they heard a horse gallop up behind them. Turning, they saw Uncle Miguel ride up.

Diego greeted his brother. "What brings you? I didn't expect to see you so soon."

Miguel gazed down from his horse. "I've joined Fremont. He's camped here."

Diego placed his hand against the shoulder of Miguel's scrawny horse. "So you decided to ride with Fremont. Where is your camp? I would like to see this army."

"The vaqueros are camped north, in the valley at the mouth of the arroyo. You'll see our fires. Come tonight and eat with us. But first, if we want dinner, I must round up some of the cattle from your rancho. See you tonight. *Adios.*"

Before dark, José rode with his papa to Fremont's campsite. Hundreds of men were camped. Few wore military uniforms. There were many buckskin-clad mountain men with coonskin caps, war-painted Indians with feathers in their long braids, and vaqueros wearing wide-brimmed hats.

Indians from different tribes kept warm around campfires while vaqueros cooked large hunks of beef on roasting sticks. The smell of the meat's juicy fat mingled with oak coals pulled them toward the camp.

"I'm looking for Miguel Rodriquez. Is he here?" Diego asked a vaquero who stood when they rode up.

"*Sí*, but he took some beef to Fremont's camp. He'll be back soon. Come, sit with us."

They hobbled their horses and turned them loose still saddled, and then joined the men around the campfire. "I'm Diego, Miguel's brother. This is my son, José. We work at this rancho."

"A fine rancho. Your beef is fat. The meat will be tasty."

The vaquero inhaled deeply, sniffing the sizzling beef as he turned a big chunk of meat over the hot coals. "It should be ready soon."

While they were talking, Miguel rode up. A tall Indian wearing a blue coat with brass buttons rode beside him. Dismounting, they unsaddled their horses and then let them loose to graze.

Diego Rodriquez stood, and the two brothers grasped hands. "I want you to meet Captain Truckee, the leader of Fremont's Indian scouts," Miguel said. "This is my brother, Diego, and his son."

José stared at the man standing next to his papa. The title Captain was only given to important men. "*Buenas noches,* Señor."

"*Buenas noches,*" Captain Truckee replied.

Colonel Fremont is asking the ranchero for beef and fresh horses," Miguel said. "The army's horses are weak and hungry from the long march." He joined the vaqueros around the campfire. "It was a hard journey from the north. With no grass, our horses are too tired to go any farther. But now it is the rainy season. The grass will grow, and our march will become easier."

José and Captain Truckee stood together, warming themselves by the hot coals. "Sit and join us," Miguel invited the Captain. "Tell my brother how you've guided white settlers into California."

Captain Truckee nodded. "I am the chief of a Paiute tribe on the other side of the great California mountains and have led white settlers over them many times." Instead of sitting, Truckee raised his chin and stood straighter. "When I was Colonel Fremont's guide, we became friends. Now, he has put me in charge of the battalion's Indian scouts."

José was amazed by how many Indians were part of the battalion. "Are all these Indians from your tribe on the other side the great mountains?"

"No. Delaware Indians came west with Fremont. A band of

Walla Walla Indians came from Oregon, and some Indians from California joined when Fremont got here. They have chiefs, but when they want something, they come to me. Then I talk to Fremont for them."

"Are the settlers and Indians friendly?" Diego asked. "I thought there was trouble between them."

"There have been misunderstandings," Captain Truckee said. "But we're all brothers, and someday, we will live in peace. When, I don't know. Perhaps when there is peace between Mexico and the United States."

Truckee nodded. "I like Americans. It will be good for California to be part of Colonel Fremont and the white settlers' country."

Captain Truckee started singing. The vaqueros loved to sing. One man picked up his guitar and began to play, and they joined in the song.

"Oh, say can you see," Captain Truckee sang loudly. The vaqueros followed along. They didn't understand the English words but laughed and tried to repeat them. Soon, voices sang out from the Indian camp.

The next morning, Miguel came to Diego's adobe to say goodbye and promised to stop on his way home. Then he spurred his horse to catch up with Fremont's vaqueros.

Later that night, pounding hoofs beat outside José's window. Looking out, he saw Uncle Miguel. His papa opened the front door, and José went to see what had happened.

"Why have you returned?" Diego asked.

"Fremont's vaqueros have stolen Santo." Miguel's dark eyes narrowed. "I thought it was a mistake, but the vaqueros laughed when I said they had taken your rancho's finest stallion and best horses. I came to tell you and help get them back."

"José get the bell mare," Diego said, pulling on his boots. "We'll go tonight and bring those horses home."

He hurriedly dressed, then saddled his horse and went to

lasso the bell mare. The bell mare was the herd leader. The young horses were trained to follow the sound of the bell she wore around her neck.

José threw a loop, caught her, and joined the other vaqueros his papa had awakened.

A rider galloped up. "Is that you, Pedro?" José asked.

"If there's a fight, you'll need me."

"Fight. Do you think there will be a fight?"

"Why not? They have stolen the horses and might not want to give them back."

Chapter Six
~ Horses in the Night~

Out into the night, Uncle Miguel led the vaqueros toward Fremont's camp. They couldn't allow someone to steal the rancho's best horses. It had taken years to train the horses to spin and stop quickly. Without well-trained horses, the vaqueros couldn't rope the wild cattle.

It was a moonless night. Surrounded by shadow riders and pounding hoofs, José, riding his favorite horse, Amigo, led the bell mare. After running for miles, Amigo panted. The horse, ribs heaving in and out, took huge breaths to fill his hungry lungs with air.

Finally, Uncle Miguel slowed his horse to a walk. "Quiet. The camp is near," he said in a low voice. "The horses are down by the stream."

José cringed when the rocks crunched under Amigos' hoofs as the vaqueros rode toward the stream. They soon found Santo and the ranchero's other favorite horses grazing along the stream's grassy edge.

"We'll scatter the herd," Diego said. "José be ready. Our horses will follow the bell mare you're leading."

"Ya, Ya, Ya-eeee. Ya, Ya, Ya-eee." The vaqueros screamed, and the startled animals ran in all directions.

"Ya, Ya, Ya-eee," José yelled, and pulled the bell mare next to the stampeding horses. The rancho's horses veered away from the others and followed the bell's familiar sound.

All the racket woke the men in Fremont's camp. Someone shouted, "Indians are stealing the horses. Get up. Get up."

Uncle Miguel rode next to José and said, "They think Indians have stolen the horses. Keep running. I'll return to Fremont's camp and say the horses ran the other way."

He turned his horse and disappeared.

José raced ahead. Although the night was cold, sweat lathered his horse's neck. Beside him, Diego yelled, "Slow down. No one is following. Give me the bell mare, and I'll lead the horses to the far side of the rancho. Go home."

José slowed his horse to a walk, and an idea jumped into his mind. This was his chance to join Fremont's battalion and earn the twenty-five dollars he promised to pay the vaqueros. His papa wouldn't miss him for a while. He could follow Fremont for a day or so before joining him. Then maybe, his uncle wouldn't send him home.

Instead of riding Amigo toward the rancho, José turned him around and rode toward Fremont's camp. For miles, under the starry night, he jogged along the grassy valley trail. Only owls hooted and coyotes howled as he passed Mission Santa Ines. It was almost morning when he reached the camp.

He dismounted. "Shhh, Amigo," he whispered from a hiding place behind the bushes. He watched as grumbling men rolled out of their warm blankets. Voices echoed around the camp. Fires were stoked. José smelled the aroma of coffee as it boiled.

Fremont's vaqueros, who still had horses, rode out looking for the escaped animals. José scrunched low in the bushes and prayed Amigo would not whinny.

Sagebrush rustled as horsemen rode around him like a swarm of bees. When a small herd of cattle rushed toward him, José mounted and urged Amigo through the brush, driving the cattle as if he was one of Fremont's vaqueros. No one noticed him.

Out in the open, he dropped behind so he wouldn't be discovered. José watched out for his uncle but didn't see him. He helped drive the cattle and horses and felt safe enough until the evening when he again hid in the bushes. It seemed like a good plan until he smelled barbequed beef. Hungry, the delicious smell and his grumbling stomach tempted him to take a chance and join the camp for dinner.

Afraid of what his uncle would do if he found out he had followed Fremont, José stayed hidden. He quietly unsaddled Amigo and tied him to a branch. He made a bed on the hard ground, wrapped in his serape.

Right now, Mama and Papa must be sitting in front of a fire, eating *frijoles* and tamales. They probably missed him, but he had to earn the money he needed. He could almost taste Mama's spicy tamales. He envied Amigo nibbling on tidbits of brush while his growling stomach kept waking him during the long, cold night.

A bugle blast from Fremont's camp woke him. The morning was cool and cloudy and smelled like rain. José worried it would not just be another hungry day, but a wet one, too.

"We can make it one more day, Amigo," he told his horse while lagging behind the vaqueros.

The trail became brushy and difficult to travel. José avoided tendrils of poison oak growing along the narrow trail. Struggling to climb the steep mountain pass, Fremont's men loudly cussed and complained as the battalion hoisted a cannon across deep arroyos.

The cattle didn't like the difficult travel either and tried to turn back. A vaquero struggling to keep the cows and horses from scattering said, "I think the cows are smarter than Fremont. Why is he taking this rugged Indian path over the steep Santa Ynez Mountains when there is an easier way?"

The vaqueros had a hard time keeping the animals together until they reached the mountain's peak. Then as they began traveling down the steep trail, it started to rain. The rain began slowly. Then lightning flashed, and thunder cracked as water pelted down from black clouds.

The drenching rain stung José's face, and almost blinded, he could hardly see the trail ahead. It rained so hard the narrow trail became like a waterfall. José dismounted and led Amigo, using the horse as a shield against the piercing storm.

The water gushed down the narrow path. Amigo almost swept off his feet, frantically scrambled to keep his footing.

"Come, Amigo. We must get off this trail, away from this rushing water." José led the terrified horse off the dangerous trail. As they climbed higher and higher over the craggy rocks, the wind and rain nearly knocked them down.

A flash of lightning revealed a cave above them. "Look, Amigo. God has provided shelter. We must climb to the safety of that cave."

José crawled, and Amigo stumbled as they scrambled up the slippery wet mountain. They reached the cave, and he led the frightened Amigo inside.

Outside, the wind and rain roared, interrupted by lightning flashes and thunderclaps that shook the ground. Cold and miserable in the darkness, José wrapped his arms around Amigo's trembling neck, trying to get warm.

He stood in the dark for a long time, hugging Amigo and shivering from the cold. Then a bright flash of lightning. Amigo turned his head and pricked his ears toward the cave's opening.

Was it just the noise of the storm or did his horse hear something outside?

"Who's out there?" he shouted.

No one answered.

Amigo's body tensed.

Something *must* be outside.

Was it a grizzly looking for shelter?

"Who's there?" he screamed louder, hoping his voice would scare away whatever was out there.

Despite the noisy storm, he heard gravelly footsteps. Something had entered the cave. "Who is it?" José called out again.

A voice replied, "Who's in here?"

"Who are you?"

"It's Pedro. Is that you, José?"

"Pedro, are you following me?" José pretended he was angry but was glad he and Amigo were no longer alone.

"I was trying to catch up with Fremont's army when this storm hit," Pedro said.

Pedro's teeth chattered from the cold and wet. Flashes of lightning lighted the cave, and José could see his dripping, wet hair, and sopping shirt.

José was just as soggy. "Get closer to Amigo. He'll keep you warm."

In the dark, Pedro edged around the trembling horse and stood near José. The boys leaned against Amigo, finding comfort from the horse's warm body and each other's company.

"Why are you here?" Pedro asked.

"I was going to join Fremont's vaqueros, too. Where is your horse?"

"He fell in the darkness. The reins slipped out of my hands, and he disappeared. I saw this cave and thought it would be a good place to stay dry. I've never seen it rain like this. I hope it stops soon. The war will be over before I catch up with Fremont."

"Papa says it's not our fight," José said. "Why do you want to join Fremont's army?"

"For the money Fremont is paying vaqueros. If I earn enough, someday, if I save it, I could buy a little rancho."

"You are a blacksmith, not a vaquero."

"Maybe so. But I have a horse, and Fremont won't know the difference. Besides, he may need a blacksmith."

"Seems you don't have a horse now," José said.

"I'll find him in the morning after this rain stops."

"You have big dreams. Owning a rancho? Me, with the twenty-five dollars, I want to buy a pair of spurs like the ranchero wears. A pair of beautiful silver spurs that is all I want."

It seemed strange. A day ago, he had been mad enough to punch Pedro's jaw. Now, in the scary darkness, something had changed, and they were again talking like friends.

"You vaqueros love fancy bits and shiny spurs. I can make silver spurs for you. Wearing the beautiful spurs I make *will* be lucky, and you will become the greatest horse trainer in all of Alta California."

"The greatest horse trainer?" To be the greatest horse trainer in Alta California had never entered José's mind. He just needed silver spurs to bring him luck and to help him become brave enough to ride the wild, bucking colts and make his papa proud. That would be enough to make him happy.

Tired, the boys sat down, leaned against the cold, stone wall and fell asleep. When they woke, it was Christmas morning. It was quiet outside. The rain had stopped. In the dawn's light, they saw strange patterns painted on the cave's rocky walls.

"Look," José said, pointing at the brightly painted designs decorating the cave. "These must be the sacred paintings Tomas said our people painted long ago. They are strange. That one looks like a snake and that one like the sun."

"What do they mean?" Pedro stood and reached up to trace the painted lines with his finger. "I've heard of these paintings but have never seen them."

"Don't touch them! Tomas says they're sacred. Spirits are here. That is why our ancestors painted this cave."

José knelt and whispered a prayer the padre had taught him. He no longer knew the prayers of the people who had painted the cave. "Our ancestors must have guided us here to protect us and help us on our journey. We should leave this cave and hurry to catch up with Fremont."

José stood and led Amigo out of the cave. "Let's go."

Chapter Seven
~ The Mission~

José, Pedro, and Amigo left the cave. Water still flowed down the trail, but compared to the previous night, it was now a trickle. Wind and rain had littered the trail with rocks and twisted branches and washed it out in many places. José carefully led Amigo around boulders and loose gravel, which slowed their travel down the steep mountain.

A few miles from the cave, they found horses that Fremont's battalion lost during the horrible rainstorm. One was still hitched and dragging a cannon behind him. Twigs were twisted in their manes and tails. Their shaggy coats, soaked from the rain, were matted with mud. Some of the horse's legs were gashed and bloody. Still able to walk, they limped along, following Amigo as if he were a bell mare.

Pedro pointed up a steep hillside. "Look, there's my horse." He climbed the slippery hill and caught his horse by the headstall. "The reins are broken, but the saddle is only wet and muddy, that is all."

They slid down the muddy slope back to the trail where José waited. José placed a loop around the horse's neck and secured the lasso to his saddle horn. "You're lucky you found him. He looks bad. Before you ride him, I'll lead him awhile to make sure that ugly cut hasn't injured his leg."

With Pedro on foot, followed by a sad-looking bunch of horses, the boys continued down the perilous trail until coming upon a landslide blocking the way. Vultures circled high above. Beneath the rubble, three dead horses lay on their backs, legs twisted, crushed by rocks.

Pedro shook his head at the ghastly sight. "Last night, we were very lucky."

"If the spirits had not guided us to their cave, we might be dead, too." José nervously looked at the rocky ledge above the slide where huge chunks of broken rocks still clung like loose teeth, threatening to tumble down.

He dismounted Amigo and silently prayed as they cautiously picked their way over the landslide's rubble that blocked the trail.

Fremont's troop of horses followed Amigo up and over the slide. It was difficult hiking over the pile of mud and broken rock. Amigo snorted and shied as José urged him past the dead horses. Many times, the boys and horses stumbled and bruised their knees.

Once over the slide, the trail became less steep, and the narrow canyon widened. Ahead lay a valley where smoke rising from campfires blended with the cloudy sky. "That must be Fremont's battalion. I smell food. Hurry." Pedro stepped in front of Amigo and ran down the slippery trail.

José smelled the tasty aroma too and remembered how long it had been since his last meal. He mounted and with his lasso still tied around Pedro's horse's neck, kicked Amigo into a trot.

Pedro leaped off the trail when he heard Amigo trot up behind him. José rushed past, and Pedro yelled, "Hey, don't leave me. You have my horse. His legs look fine. I want to ride."

José turned and rode back. Pedro checked his cinch and hoisted himself into the saddle. He barely had time to climb on before José kicked Amigo. He grabbed the saddle horn as his horse sprinted down the mountain at a gallop.

At the campsite, Indians sat around a fire. They were surprised when two bedraggled boys raced into their camp followed by a small bunch of loose horses, one pulling a rattling, bouncing cannon.

José slid his horse to a muddy stop. "*Buenos días, amigos.* Is this Colonel Fremont's camp?"

"One of the Indians said, "Captain Truckee is camped over there, at the big tree." He pointed to a huge oak about a quarter of a mile away.

"We're very hungry, Señor," Pedro said. "We have not eaten in days. Do you have a little meat to spare?"

The Indian nodded. "Take what you want. We have plenty."

"*Gracias.*" José jumped off his horse, smacked his lips, grabbed a chunk of stringy meat off the coals, and sat by the fire to eat. "This meat tastes sweet, different from the beef at our rancho."

"It's not beef," the Indian said.

"Venison?"

"No. This morning, we found a horse with a broken leg."

José's stomach knotted. He had never eaten horseflesh. It could be one of the horses he had ridden on the rancho. Even though he knew the Indians ate it, it didn't seem right somehow. He spat into the fire and didn't feel hungry anymore.

"Pedro, I'm riding to the tree to talk to Captain Truckee. You want to go?"

"Wait for me," Pedro said, wiping his mouth on his damp shirtsleeve. "Just let me dry my shirt by the fire."

"No, we must hurry and talk to Fremont and join his vaqueros before Uncle Miguel finds out we're here. We can get warm later." José picked up his reins and threw them around Amigo's neck. He mounted, and then firmly tied the rope on Pedro's horse to his saddle horn.

Pedro frowned. "I'm tired of being led like a child. Does anyone have extra reins?"

The Indians didn't seem to understand. They grinned and shook their heads. José shrugged. "Get on your horse, Pedro. At least you don't have to walk."

Pedro climbed on his horse, and they trotted about a quarter of a mile to the tree where Captain Truckee camped. They saw his blue coat, rode to where he sat near a fire, and dismounted.

"*Buenos días,* Captain," José said. "Do you remember us? We met at a rancho north of here."

Captain Truckee nodded. "I remember you. Miguel is your uncle. I know him well. He is away with the vaqueros looking for the horses and the cannon we lost last night in that awful rainstorm. We're lucky to be alive this morning."

"Many of Fremont's horses followed us out of the canyon. One is hitched to a cannon." José pointed. "They're at the camp back there."

The exhausted men sat around a fire. Their eyes were empty, vacant like the eyes of horses run too far and too fast. José wondered how he looked. His hat felt like a limp rag on his head, the eagle feather in its hatband blown away by the wind. His clothes were damp, and he shivered with cold.

Pedro stood by the campfire warming his backside. José got nearer the fire, sat down, and asked, "Where is Colonel Fremont camped? We want to join his vaqueros and would like to talk to him."

"He and the battalion are setting up camp in Santa Barbara," Captain Truckee said. "No one was at the Presidio to defend the town. All the townsmen left to ambush us at the Gaviota Pass. They thought we were going that way."

Captain Truckee gazed at the gray sky. "Lucky for us Fremont's trick worked. Except he didn't expect it to be such a terrible journey. If the men loyal to Mexico *had been* waiting in Santa Barbara, after climbing over that mountain pass last night, we had no strength left to fight."

"We were lucky last night too. The spirits led us to a cave." José's shirt began to dry as he told his story.

Around noon, after drying their damp clothing, Pedro asked, "Does anyone have a rope? Or anything I can use for reins?"

"No, everything was lost in the storm. Maybe one of the vaqueros in Santa Barbara will have reins. I'm going there. You can ride with me," Captain Truckee offered.

Captain Truckee and the boys rode out. With José still leading Pedro on his horse, they traveled south toward the angry, gray Pacific Ocean and into Santa Barbara. José was awed by the large gardens and the size of the white adobes scattered along the dirt road leading toward the Presidio in the center of town.

In town, they heard music. "What's going on?" José asked.

Captain Truckee laughed. "I know that tune. It is 'Yankee Doodle.' There is Fremont." He pointed. "Your uncle is with him."

With flutes, drums and fiddles, a group of Indians marched from the mission down the main road toward the beach playing "Yankee Doodle" over and over. Colonel Fremont sat on his horse, reviewing them as they passed. A few men sat horseback beside him.

José squinted. One of the men did look like his uncle. "This could be trouble," he whispered to Pedro. "Uncle Miguel will spoil our plans. What should we do?"

"They have seen us and are riding this way," Pedro said. "It is too late to disappear now."

When he rode up, José's uncle asked, "What are you doing here? Has something happened? Did your papa send you?"

José stared at the ground, his tongue stuck to the roof of his dry mouth.

"No, Señor," Pedro spoke quickly. "I have come to join Fremont. I want to help him claim Alta California."

Uncle Miguel narrowed his eyes. "Have you come with your papa's approval? Or perhaps not. Is that it? Eh, José? Does your papa know you are here?"

José raised his chin, nodded, and tried to think of what to say.

Uncle Miguel's voice became gruff. "He will be worried. Both of you must go back to the rancho. A war is no place for you."

Colonel Fremont nodded. "I agree with your uncle. I want no trouble from your angry fathers. They will hold me responsible. No, you must go home. Although I must say, you were brave to have made it here during that storm."

José straightened his shoulders and sat taller on Amigo. "*Sí,* Colonel. We spent the night in a cave." He said nothing about how much the thunder and lightning had frightened him.

Colonel Fremont turned his attention to Uncle Miguel. "I don't want any problems. Make sure these two go back home. And as to the beef, I have spoken to the rancheros. Go gather the cattle they sold me for the battalion."

"*Sí,* Colonel," Uncle Miguel said.

Fremont spurred his horse and rode toward the Presidio.

"You heard him, José. No trouble. Tomorrow, after you've rested your horses, you will return home. Come, we'll ride to the vaquero camp."

Chapter Eight
~ Spies~

The vaquero's camp was just outside of town. Vaqueros sat around campfires, propping their sodden boots near the flames. With crumpled, damp hats pulled low on their foreheads, they looked as miserable as José felt.

Meat sizzled on the fire. "You hungry, eh?" Uncle Miguel asked.

Worried it might be another horse steak, José said, "What's cooking?"

A vaquero snickered. "The rich ranchos have supplied us with fat beeves. We didn't bother to look for a brand, so we don't know who to thank for breakfast."

Fat dripped on the coals, and the aroma drifted to José's nostrils. He piled his plate with *frijoles* and steak. After eating his fill, he sat with the other vaqueros next to the fire, planting his feet near the flames to dry his damp boots. Exhausted, he soon fell asleep.

The next morning, laughter woke him. Still half asleep, he slowly became aware that the fire was now blazing, and his feet felt hot. He looked down at his steaming boots and jumped up, then hopped from foot to foot.

The vaqueros laughed. "Hot foot, eh?"

José felt foolish until he noticed other vaqueros had removed their boots and left them too close to the fire also. He pointed to their smoldering boots. "Looks like some of you will be barefoot." He laughed when the vaqueros rushed to fish their boots out of the fire with a stick.

He found Pedro sound asleep, his head covered with a saddle blanket. "Pedro, wake up."

Pedro rolled over and yawned. "What for? Why hurry?"

"I want to leave early. I don't want to face Uncle Miguel this morning."

"I'm not ready to go back over that awful mountain."

"We can ride back the easier way, along the coast trail, and through the mountains at the Gaviota Pass."

"Isn't that where men from Santa Barbara wait to ambush Fremont?" Pedro gazed over José's shoulder, frowned, and said, "*Hola*, Señor Miguel."

José spun around, and his uncle stood in front of him.

"Get up, Pedro. No time to sleep. Get ready and go home. Your papas will be worried. We were lucky. The battalion met no resistance here. As soon as they reorganize, we'll be marching south."

The boys gobbled their breakfast and then saddled their horses. "I need reins for my bridle," Pedro complained. "I can't be led all the way back to the rancho."

"Ask Uncle Miguel," José said.

When Pedro asked, Uncle Miguel said, "We have nothing to spare. We lost many horses and equipment in that rainstorm. Today, I must go back up the mountain and find the cannon and stray horses. You better hurry and get going before Fremont decides he needs *your* horses."

"Some of Fremont's horses followed us down the mountain," José said. "One even pulled a cannon. They're at the camp near the mouth of the pass."

"I will get them. Remember, when you get home, tell your papa it was your idea to follow Fremont. I don't want any blame for this." Uncle Miguel urged the boys to hurry and gave them strips of jerky to eat on the way.

As the boys rode out of camp, Pedro scowled when the vaqueros laughed and waved good-bye. "They think I am a fool that needs someone to lead my horse."

A jackrabbit bounded in front of the horses as they plodded slowly north along the level coastal trail. The plateau stretched for miles between mountains that lifted sharply toward the sky and ocean cliffs that dropped to a sandy beach. Beyond the beach, a foggy haze hugged the murky water.

"Are you sure it's safe going this way?" Pedro asked. "What if the Mexican army is still waiting for Fremont at Gaviota?"

"If they see us, just say we're vaqueros."

"Maybe we shouldn't go home at all," Pedro said. "On the way, we could find a job on another rancho."

Too surprised to reply, José had never thought of working anywhere except the rancho where he grew up, where his papa worked. But maybe it was a good idea. Returning to the rancho wasn't as exciting as leaving it. And he didn't want to face his angry papa. If he didn't go home, he wouldn't have to worry about pleasing him, or being brave enough to ride the wild horses.

The horses walked side-by-side in an easy rhythm.

Tired, José closed his eyes. No worry; Amigo knew the way home. He didn't know how long he'd napped, when Pedro yelled, "Wake up. The horses have found a good place to make camp."

José opened his eyes to the glow of a foggy-pink sun setting over the ocean. The horses had stopped to graze by a small, wooded stream where broad-limbed oak trees provided shelter. He dismounted. "Let's gather wood and make a fire."

The wind blew, and it threatened to rain as they unsaddled their horses, hobbled them, and searched for wood dry enough to burn. By the time they'd gathered wood, it had grown dark. Lighting the fire was difficult, but they took turns blowing on bits of twigs and moss until a small blaze flared.

The boys crowded next to the smoky fire and ate the tough jerky. "Chewing jerky makes my jaws ache," Pedro said.

Glad to have something to eat, José didn't complain. He kept gnawing on the strips of salty beef. Amigo nickered. "What is it, boy? Do you hear something?"

Brush crackled as if something prowled in the shadows. Or was it just the wind?

José stood and quickly looked around. "Hear that, Pedro? If it's a grizzly, we should climb a tree."

Then brush crackled all around them. Which way should they go?

Pedro jumped to his feet, eyes wide, ready to run.

José's heart dropped to his stomach when out of the bushes horsemen charged into the firelight and surrounded them.

With a dirty bandanna tied around his head and a menacing gleam in his eyes, a man who seemed to be the leader pointed a pistol at José. "Who are you?" he yelled. "Why are you here? Are you Fremont's spies?"

José's mind spun. The taste of spicy jerky coated his dry tongue and soured in his mouth. These must be the men Fremont was trying to avoid by riding over the treacherous mountain pass—men fighting for Mexico.

"Well, who are you?" the leader repeated. "Why are you here? Talk!"

José cleared the salty lump in his throat and tried to gather his courage. In a trembling voice he said, "We're from Rancho Grande, looking for strays."

The leader squinted his wrinkled eyes. "In a rainstorm? Strays? You don't look like vaqueros." The man laughed. "But you don't act like spies. Lighting a fire? What kind of a spy lights a fire? A stupid one, maybe."

He spurred his dapple-gray horse and threw a lasso around Amigo's neck. Another horseman caught Pedro's horse. "Saddle your horses. We'll go to our rancho. The ranchero will decide who you are."

José and Pedro saddled their horses. Once mounted, their arms were twisted behind their backs, and their hands tightly bound.

The rope gnawed into José's wrists. Surrounded by horsemen, wind stung his eyes as they galloped to the rancho. Once at the ranchero's *casa*, the boys were roughly jerked off their horses, dragged across the yard, and tied to a post. The leader went inside the *casa*, leaving a guard to watch them.

Trying to think of what to do, José's mind raced. He whispered to Pedro, "Say nothing except that we're looking for strays."

"Shut up," the guard yelled.

Time crawled. José's hands became numb from the tight ropes. Waiting in the drizzly mist made him jittery. What was taking so long? Why didn't the ranchero come outside? When he did, what would he do to them?

Finally, a door slammed, and the ranchero appeared. The leader stood beside him and pointed his finger at the boys. "Look what we found camped by the stream. They say they're from Rancho Grande. What do you think? Maybe they're spies."

The ranchero shook his head. "Your rancho is a day's ride away. Why are you two wandering around here at night?"

José's tongue froze. It felt like Señor Eduardo's hammer beat inside his chest.

"Answer!" the leader yelled.

Pedro looked at José. He gulped and took a deep breath. "My papa sent me to look for strays. Pedro's horse fell and broke the reins. We thought his horse might be hurt, so we decided to camp and then ride back to our rancho in the morning."

Minutes ticked by as the ranchero stared at them. "Strays, huh? You are a long way from your rancho to be looking for strays."

"We got lost in the rainstorm," José said.

"Bring the lantern closer," the ranchero said. The lantern was brought nearer, and he peered at the boys' faces.

José lowered his eyes and refused to look up. With his meaty hand, the ranchero grabbed José's chin, forcing him to gaze into his black eyes. With the ranchero's face inches away, José smelled garlic on his breath. "What is your name, boy?"

The ranchero's fingers still held his chin. José could hardly open his mouth to mumble, "Uh, I… José, uh…Rodriquez."

The ranchero scowled and released José's chin. "Are you Diego Rodriquez's son?"

José nodded. Then the ranchero turned to Pedro. "What about you, eh? Do you have a name?"

Sweat trickled down Pedro's face. His voice cracked when he answered, "Pedro Garcia."

"Isn't your papa the blacksmith who was just here working for me? Eh?"

Pedro sighed. *"Sí."*

After a long silence, the ranchero said, "I suppose you're telling the truth." He turned to Pedro. "I know your papa. He is a good man, a fine blacksmith. I choose to believe you. There is a war going on. You shouldn't be wandering around. You could be mistaken for spies."

Before going back into his *casa*, he instructed the guard. "Untie them. They can camp here tonight. In the morning, send them home. Pedro, when you get home, tell your papa I send my regards. *Buenas noches.*"

After the ranchero left, the guard leered at the boys. "I don't believe your story. You're lucky. If it were up to me, you'd be hanged as spies. I will let you go, but tomorrow when you leave, never let me see you on this rancho again." As an added warning, as if it were a knife, he raked his finger across his throat and laughed.

Jose' was thankful when the guard untied his throbbing wrists. After unsaddling their horses, the boys rolled up in their saddle blankets to stay warm.

Not far away, waves rumbled, sounding like threatening voices mumbling in the darkness. It was difficult to fall asleep, and Amigos' slightest sneeze or snort woke José.

Early the next morning, the boys hurriedly saddled, then galloped from the rancho. Fear of hanging or having his throat slit kept José pushing the horses faster and faster. He had no money for a pair of silver spurs, but at least he wasn't swinging from an oak branch. Facing his angry papa seemed less threatening now.

After climbing the mountains near the Gaviota Pass, they came to Mission Santa Ines. Its cracked and crumbling adobe walls were a welcome sight.

Now, having traveled far enough to feel safe, José dismounted to rest the sweating, panting horses under the shade of an oak.

While they rested, he pulled jerky from his pack. The boys sat under the tree, munching the dry beef. Between bites, Pedro said, "I hope we don't cross more ranchos loyal to the Mexican government. We might not be lucky a second time."

"Don't worry. I know the vaqueros on this rancho. They're friendly. We'll make it home by dark."

After resting, they climbed on their horses and continued their journey. As José rode toward home, he remembered how scared he'd been when the Mexican loyalists had threatened him. He talked his way out of trouble and kept his mouth shut about Fremont but had not acted bravely. He *must* conquer his fear. Otherwise, how could he measure up when he rode the wild colts?

"My papa will be mad when I get home," Pedro said. "We

should make up a good story. Not tell them we tried to join Fremont. What do you say?"

Reminded his papa would also be unhappy, José tried to forget his worry and sat straighter in the saddle. "We've been gone for days. What good reason could we give? Besides, Uncle Miguel knows. They'd be sure to find out. Then they'd be even angrier that we lied. Telling the truth is better. Maybe our papas will be glad we've returned safely, and we will be forgiven."

Chapter Nine
~ Back at the Rancho~

It was dark and starting to rain by the time José and Pedro reached Rancho Grande. Lantern light guided them toward the barn door. Inside, they found Tomas brushing Santo's golden coat. José dismounted and touched the old man's shoulder.

Surprised, Tomas spun around. He picked up the lantern and held it up to see. "Oh, it is you, José. Are you all right? Where have you been?" Then he noticed Pedro standing behind José in the dim light. "Pedro? Is that you?"

"It is."

Before José answered Tomas's questions, he asked, "Is my papa mad?"

"Mad? Should he be mad? We thought you were dead. Everyone has been searching for you. Your papa has gone out every morning looking. Even in that terrible rainstorm, he was out looking." Tomas grasped Amigo's reins. "Go now. Hurry and let your papa know you have returned. I'll take care of your horses."

When José entered his family's small, two-room *casa*, his little sister raced over, threw her arms around his waist, and began crying.

Mama looked up from her sewing, jumped up, and shouted, "Diego, come. José is home."

His papa rushed in from the other room. "My prayers have been answered." He grabbed José's shoulder and pulled him over by the fire. "What happened? I searched everywhere for you. Are you hurt?"

José's face grew warm. "Uh, I...I'm fine. Tomas said you thought I might be hurt. I'm sorry. I never meant to cause you to worry."

"Where have you been?"

"On the night we rescued our horses from Fremont's vaqueros, I decided to follow them to join Uncle Miguel and work as a vaquero."

"And?"

"It rained, and Pedro and I found shelter in a cave. It was very cold."

"Pedro was with you?"

José's feet were damp and cold, but his face began to sweat as he gazed at his papa and saw anger spark in his eyes. "He wanted to join Fremont, too. We caught up with Fremont, but Uncle Miguel made him send us back."

"Pedro returned with you?"

"*Sí*, Papa."

"Thank God." Diego frowned. "You were foolish. You're no longer a child. It is time to think like a man. Your mama and I were worried. Pedro's papa was worried." He squeezed José's shoulder. "We've spent days riding the rancho looking for you, afraid you were killed by Fremont's men, or lying hurt somewhere." He shook his head, becoming angrier as he spoke. "So foolish."

"I'm sorry." José knew he had disappointed his papa. Ashamed to look in his eyes, he stared down at the hard-packed dirt floor.

His mama grasped his elbow, pulled him into a chair by the fire, and patted his shoulder. "You are wet and must be hungry. I will get you something to eat."

It felt good to be warm and safe, sitting with his family. His sister rolled dough out round and flat while Mama browned tortillas in an iron pan. Like his younger sister did now, José used to help his mama make tortillas. That changed when he grew older and his father directed his chores. Then he began helping with the horses and cattle, chopping wood and carrying it into the house. While he was gone, the wood stacked near the fire had dwindled.

His mama served him. Dipping a tortilla into a bowl of hot beans, he took a bite and smacked his lips. "These are the best *frijoles* I've ever tasted."

"You are hungry." His mama laughed and gave her husband a warning look, a look that saved José from harsh punishment. When Mama's eyes flashed, Papa never argued. She placed a dry change of clothes on the back of his chair. "Get dry and rest. We're glad you're home."

Wrapped in a blanket, he stretched out on his cot close to the fire and quickly fell asleep.

In the morning, inside the vaquero's adobes, morning prayers greeted the day with songs of praise. Voices joined in as the women awoke. In the other room, his mama's sweet voice trilled the prayers like a songbird.

José stretched. His sister slept across the room, her head covered with a blanket. He crawled out from under his covers and stoked last night's embers into flames. His boots were now dry, and he pulled them on.

His mama came in from the other room and said, "How do you feel this morning?"

"*Muy bien*. It is good to be home. Last night, Tomas said he would care for the horses, but I better go see to them."

The morning sun had pushed the rain clouds from the sky. In the barn, Amigo and Pedro's horse were tied next to the oxen. José looked around but didn't see Tomas. He went outside just as Pedro strolled toward the barn.

"Was your papa angry?" Pedro asked.

"*Sí*. I will be splitting firewood for a long time."

"Mine is angry too. Since he spent days hunting for us, he is behind in his work. I'll be busy helping him catch up. I better turn my horse out to pasture. Do you want me to take Amigo?"

"No, leave him tied." José followed Pedro back into the barn, and now found Tomas inside.

"*Buenos días*, boys," Tomas greeted them. "Is all well with you this morning? Tell me what happened while you were gone."

"Sorry, I have no time to talk. I must help Papa." Pedro untied his horse and led him outside.

"What about you, José?"

"Papa is angry. He said I didn't think wisely."

Tomas tottered outside to sit by the fire. José joined him and sat next to the old man.

"What happened?" Tomas squinted at José. "Where were you?"

"I wanted to earn the twenty-five dollars Uncle Miguel said Fremont was paying vaqueros. I didn't think about how worried everyone would be. I guess I didn't think at all."

"You went to join Fremont's battalion?"

"*Sí.* I rode over the mountain pass and got caught in a terrible storm. Amigo, Pedro, and I spent the night in a cave. I think the spirits guided us there. In the morning, I saw paintings in the cave. Paintings like you said our people painted long ago."

"Paintings? You spent the night in a sacred cave of our ancestors?" Tomas's eyes got a faraway gleam.

José shivered. "It was a miracle we found it. Finding that cave saved us. The next morning, many horses lay dead on the trail, killed by a landslide. It was terrible."

"You joined Fremont?"

He shook his head. "Uncle Miguel wouldn't let us. He sent us home."

"Miguel was right. You should not have gone without asking your papa."

"If I had asked, he would have said no."

"He would have," Tomas said. "But if you are man enough to go to war, then you should be man enough to tell your papa you are going."

"On the way home, we were captured. I was man enough to get out of that." Angry at Tomas's words, José spit in the fire. He shook his head and scowled. Remembering how afraid he'd been when surrounded and taken prisoner, he became angry with himself.

A real vaquero wouldn't have been scared. A vaquero never worried about danger.

"Captured?" Tomas asked.

"*Sí,* by men at the Gaviota Rancho fighting for Mexico."

"You're lucky to be back," Tomas said. "Spirits were protecting you. They must have led you to their cave because they have something to tell you. We must go to the valley of the sacred rock and seek the spirits. It is time."

Chapter Ten
~ The Vision~

During the cold winter months, many calves and foals were born. Cattle and horses gathered in wind-protected arroyos where rainwater rushed down and collected in shallow pools. José and his papa rode into one of these arroyos to check on how the young animals were doing.

José pointed at a golden filly. "Isn't she beautiful, Papa?" He rode closer to the foal. He enjoyed seeing the newborn animals, so small, yet so tough.

The mare, protecting her foal, snorted a warning and pawed the ground. "Look out, José. Don't get too close," Diego yelled.

An angry mama cow was dangerous, but mares also became angry when their foal was threatened. They kept close watch over their foals, using hooves and teeth instead of horns to defend against predators, even challenging vaqueros who came too close. José was amazed by how a mare herd banded together to fight an enemy. Once, he had even seen them fighting a cougar.

He turned from watching the horses and scanned his papa's face. "Tomas often talks about the sacred rock, but I've never journeyed there. He wants to visit the valley of the sacred rock before the spring rodeo and thinks I should go with him to seek a vision. What do you think, Papa?"

"The rock. Tomas visits it often. He still believes his mama's old stories about the spirits. It is good. You should go. When does he want to leave?"

"In a few days." José was surprised that his papa approved. He never spoke about the old ways like Tomas.

When they returned to the rancho, growing eager to seek a

vision, José hurried to find Tomas. "Papa said I could go with you."

Tomas looked up from his work and then carefully laid the strings of rawhide aside. *"Muy bueno.* Are you ready? It's a two-day ride. We'll get supplies and start our journey tomorrow. We will take your bull hide. It will help you with your vision."

He looked at the hide, tanned, and safely hanging high in the barn's rafters. Pedro was wrong. Tomas was right. Chaps made from this hide would be lucky.

Early the next morning, he saddled Amigo and helped Tomas saddle a mule. They packed jerky and water, and then followed the trail toward the inland valley. Amigo plodded beside the old man's mule. If he had been riding alone, Jose would have kicked his horse into a fast gallop. But because of Tomas's old injury, they traveled at a slow pace.

Tomas was quiet, staring straight ahead. He usually told stories. After riding a few miles, his silence began to bother José. "What is wrong? Are you angry with me, Tomas?"

"No. I'm thinking. Our journey is a time to honor and remember our ancestors. I think of my mama. I'm getting old, and my memory is not so good." Tomas frowned and looked at the sky. "It's hard to remember what she told me about our people before the padres came, and everything changed."

The rolling foothill trail became steep. Tomas urged his mule up the rugged path. Halfway up the slope, he stopped to rest the panting animals and looked back down at the valley.

It was a clear day. José twisted in his saddle to see the view. Beyond the level land below, miles of white dunes stretched along the blue-green ocean. His home looked different from here. He felt small looking down at the vast valley and couldn't imagine anything more beautiful.

"It is paradise, eh?" Tomas said. "Every time I ride this trail, I'm awed by this sight."

They continued the trek up and up the steep, zigzagging mountain trail. One unsure hoofstep and horse and rider could topple down the rocky mountainside. Finally reaching the summit, they again stopped to view the vista below, not speaking for a long time.

The steep mountains turned into gently rolling hills again that were easier for the animals to climb. José and the old man traveled until sunset. In an arroyo, they dismounted and prepared for the night. Oaks grew on the sides of the arroyo, making it easy for José to gather wood for the campfire.

"Make a big fire," Tomas said. "We don't need grizzlies in camp tonight."

José tied Amigo, and then gathered dry branches, breaking them into small pieces. He dug a shallow pit and cleared a place for the fire. Soon, a small blaze crackled.

Tomas unpacked water and jerky, and they ate, seated near the fire. For a long time, they stared into the flames, enjoying the silence, broken only by an owl's hoot.

The next morning, Tomas motioned. "Come with me."

Not knowing what to expect, José followed him. Not far from camp, in a rocky grotto, a pool bubbled up, and steam wafted from a hot spring.

"We must bathe and prepare for our vision," Tomas said. In the cold morning air, he tugged off his boots and undressed down to his baggy underwear. Entering the spring, he sat in hot water up to his chin and closed his eyes. José also removed his boots and clothing, and shivering, quickly climbed in beside him.

The steamy water soon made his forehead drip with sweat. They soaked in the warm water until Tomas opened his eyes, climbed out of the pool, and quickly dressed.

José didn't move. He had no desire to leave the warmth of the spring into the cold air. "*Pronto. Pronto*," Tomas yelled. "It is time to go."

He crept out of the warm water, swiftly dressed, and pulled his boots onto his wet feet. Back at the camp, he threw dirt on the coals of last night's fire.

They gathered the animals, saddled and bridled them, then packed the blankets and water.

"Now we're ready," the old man said.

José helped Tomas onto his mule. Once on the trail, they rode east through groves of oaks, following a brushy deer path. By midday, the mountains behind them, the groves of trees disappeared, and the weather grew cooler. Straight ahead in the distance, a lone rock perched in a flat, windy valley.

Riding another hour, they arrived at the base of the gigantic mound of stone. José was amazed by the rock's size. Irregular holes pockmarked its otherwise smooth surface. No nearby tree or hill offset its abrupt rise from the earth. As they rode around it, lizards scurried into cracks. On the rock's eastern side, a large opening loomed.

"This is a very sacred place," Tomas said. "Inside are mysterious paintings. When I was your age, my mama brought me here to seek a vision." He slowly dismounted his mule and stretched his back. "This may be my last visit."

Eager to see inside the cave, José hurriedly dismounted and started to go inside. Tomas put his hand on José's shoulder. "Wait, don't enter yet. Help me." He then helped unload the packs and a bundle of sage Tomas had gathered along the trail.

Tomas clutched the sage against his chest. "Even though she was baptized into the Church, my mama taught me to revere all the spirits. She said the padre became angry if our people worshiped in the old ways and would punish them."

He made the sign of the cross and blessed himself. "No matter. She believed in the spirits, the saints, and the Holy Ghost. She feared them all. I'm getting old and cannot remember all the rituals she taught me." He lowered his voice to a whisper. "But I do remember when I came here for my first vision. Bring the bull hide and follow me."

José pulled the hide off the mule and followed Tomas as he carried the sage inside the cave. Through an opening in the rocky roof, a shaft of sunlight pierced the center of the large cave.

Strange figures were painted on the walls in brilliant red, black, and white. Tomas laid a clump of sage into a recess in the cave's wall blackened by many fires.

"Go, gather firewood," Tomas said. "When you return, we will prepare ourselves for our vision."

He mounted Amigo to search for firewood, riding back through the hills they had just passed. It took a long time to find enough wood.

When José returned dragging a bundle of wood behind his horse, Tomas was singing a strange song he had never heard. The old man's voice rose and fell in an unfamiliar language. José entered the cave and laid the firewood in a pile, then knelt next to Tomas and quietly waited.

"We must seek our dreams," Tomas said. "Yours for the first time, mine for the last. I will ask the Great Spirit to send a dream helper to give you knowledge. In this cave, you will fast and seek your dream helper."

Tomas folded his hands and closed his eyes. "If you have a vision, you will gain power, but you must use this power to help people. You must have an unselfish reason for seeking a vision or your dream helper won't come."

"What is the song you were singing?" José asked.

"It is a prayer to the spirits, the saints, and the Holy Ghost. I'm asking them to send a dream helper to guide you. Here, let's make a purifying fire, to cleanse and ready us to travel into the spirit world."

"Is the song in the language of our people?" José had heard the Indians at the rancho speak the Chumash language, but had never learned it. He only spoke Spanish.

"*Sí.*" Tomas nodded. "So much has changed. Many of our people have died or moved to live with other tribes. We have lost memories of how things used to be. Now sit and I will light the fire."

Tomas lighted the fire and placed sage on the flames. The cave filled with a strong, woody aroma as thick smoke rose through its roof's natural chimney. Again, the old man chanted.

"Sing with me, José," he said.

José tried to imitate the song's words, and together they sang to the spirits in their ancient tongue.

After singing awhile, Tomas spread the rest of the sage on the cave's soft earthen floor and then placed the bull hide over the fragrant, brushy bed. "Here you will sleep and seek your dream helper. The hide will be your bed. The great and brave bull will help you on your journey. Now, I go and seek my vision. Stay here until my return. I will take your horse. *Adios*."

Tomas rose and limped out of the cave, leaving José no food or water. He shivered, sat and waited. It grew dark. Through the opening to the sky, the stars started to twinkle overhead.

What was he supposed to do to seek his dream helper? He knelt and began to sing the song Tomas had taught him. Even though he didn't know the meaning of the words, he sang on and on until he grew tired. Lying on the hide, he wrapped it around his body to keep warm, and then fell asleep.

A noise outside the cave woke him. It sounded like a hungry animal sniffing his scent. Was it coyotes, or worse, a grizzly? Fear, he felt fear. José held his breath trying to hear, but his heart pounded too loudly in his ears.

After a few minutes, his heartbeat slowed, and all seemed quiet. He rolled onto his back and opened his eyes. The cave was dark but seen through the opening above stars filled the sky. He felt alone. Here in this place where so many had come to seek their vision, he felt no bigger than a grain of sand.

He began to sing. If he was going to die tonight, José wanted to die singing his people's sacred song. Besides, perhaps the spirits might help him.

He stopped singing, listened, and still heard nothing outside. Maybe it had been an evil spirit, and his song had driven it away. Feeling safer, José fell asleep.

He woke as the sun began to light the sky and chase the stars out of the heavens. His stomach growled. Wrapping the bull hide around his shoulders, he got up to look out the cave's opening.

Outside, a thick mist lingered on the ground. The dense fog formed gray shadows. José stretched out his arm and couldn't see farther than his hand. He thought he heard hoof beats. "Is that you, Tomas? Are you there?"

No answer. José wished it were the old man. He wished he could have a drink of water and a piece of tough jerky to quiet his rumbling stomach.

He listened. Nothing. What should he do? The whole day loomed ahead. He could think only of his hunger and thirst.

"Why have I come here?" Hearing his voice felt strange. "Now I am talking to myself."

Throwing more wood on the fire, he added some of the sage Tomas had placed under the bull hide to the flames.

Again, smoke filled the cave. Again, José sang.

He didn't know how long he had been singing before he heard a shrill whinny outside the cave. He looked out, and there in the thick mist was Santo.

He was glad to see the beautiful golden horse. "How did you get here? Eh? Did you follow us? Come inside the cave, Santo."

The stallion followed José inside. Next to the flames, the firelight made his golden coat glisten. Now with Santo there, he was no longer lonely. He leaned against the horse's strong shoulder.

The horse turned his head and stared at him. His eyes blazed like burning coals. "José, I have come with a message."

Amazed, José stepped back. Had Santo spoken?

Santo walked to the cave's entrance, snorted, and again turned to look at José. He followed the horse outside.

The fog was gone, and the sun was shining. "Look at the mountains," Santo instructed.

He looked, and the distant mountains glimmered like gold.

Santo said, "Do not follow the gold into the mountains. Gold only brings death. Always remember, you are a vaquero."

José glanced at the beautiful horse. When he looked back at

the mountains, they no longer glimmered. "I don't understand, Santo."

"You will know when you know," Santo replied. "Until then, remember."

He turned to ask more questions, but Santo had disappeared. It was nighttime, and the fog had returned. José stood for a long time staring at the spot where Santo had been.

When he went back into the cave, the fire was barely alive, so he placed more wood on the coals. He threw the last branches of sage on the flames and once again sang his people's prayer, no longer bothered by hunger or thirst. All that night he waited for Santo's return.

Still lying wrapped in his bull hide blanket, a voice woke José from the place of distant dreams. He opened his eyes.

Tomas's face floated above. Peering at José, he shook his shoulder. "Are you awake?"

"I think so. Maybe. I'm not sure. Is that really you, Tomas?" José gazed at him, not sure if he was still dreaming.

"It is me. You must be hungry after your fast. Come help me unload the mule. I've brought food and water. It has been three days since I left you. Let's eat. I'm hungry, too."

Wearing his bull hide cloak, he followed Tomas out of the cave. The morning was cold, the sun just rising above the rim of the mountains.

Amigo was tied to the mule. "Amigo, how are you?" José asked. The horse didn't answer.

He unloaded jerky and water off the mule's pack and took it inside the cave. Tomas threw wood on the fire and they sat near its heat. Neither spoke.

Tomas gave him water and a piece of the tough dried meat.

Starved and thirsty José said, "This jerky tastes better than anything I've ever eaten."

Tomas smiled. "Hunger brings out the flavor, eh?"

The flickering flames made the paintings on the cave walls dance and come alive. José stared at the red images, shadowed and outlined with black and white. "Who painted these walls?"

"I don't know. They were painted long ago, before I was born." Tomas's eyes never left the fire. "It may have been a hundred years or a thousand years ago."

José wished he knew more about these people who had left their mark on this cave's walls. The paintings made him aware of his people's long history. A people he would never know. Sadness filled him.

"We should return now," Tomas said in a voice that sounded far away. "It is time to load our things and start back to the rancho."

"Last night, I saw Santo," José said.

"Santo wouldn't have traveled so far. It could not have been Santo. Maybe it was one of the mustangs that roam this valley." Tomas began gathering the things, preparing to leave.

"I heard him speak. He knew me. He knew my name."

"Speak, eh?" Tomas raised his scraggly eyebrows. "It was your dream helper. He came in a familiar form so you wouldn't be afraid. I've come here every year seeking a vision since I was your age, but I've never had one. I'm glad you have. You're very lucky."

"He told me not to follow gold into the mountains. What does it mean? Do you know, Tomas?"

"No," the old man said. "Is that all he told you?"

"Santo said, 'You will know when you know.' That is all." José hoped Tomas would understand.

Tomas nodded. "When you are ready you will know what the spirits revealed. Always remember your vision, pray and think about it. This knowledge will give you power when needed. Now get your bull hide. It is time to go home."

Chapter Eleven
~ Spurs~

On their way back to the rancho, when they got to the hot spring, Tomas halted his mule. "We'll enjoy these springs tonight. The hot water eases my stiff leg after spending so many hours in the saddle."

José made camp, gathered wood, and then joined Tomas soaking in the hot pool. He gazed at the stars and wondered about his vision. "Tomas, is there gold in the mountains?"

"There must be. I've heard stories about gold. Indians never had a use for it, but the Spanish loved gold."

That night, José slept soundly and had no dreams. In the morning, continuing their journey trekking down the mountain, they again viewed the white dunes and sparkling ocean in the endless yonder.

After the steep descent, eager to reach the rancho, the animals walked swiftly, knowing that home wasn't too far. José heard hoofs tromping behind him and twisted in his saddle to see a man approaching at a gallop.

"Tomas, someone is coming."

The man slid his horse to a stop a few feet away, creating a dusty cloud. Tomas halted his mule, squinting his eyes to see.

José was surprised to see his uncle. "Why have you left Fremont's battalion? Do you have news about the war? Is it over?"

"I do have news." Uncle Miguel smiled. "How are you, Tomas? Where are you two going?"

"We aren't going," Tomas said. "We're coming. We journeyed to the valley of the sacred rock. It was time for José to seek his vision."

Uncle Miguel scowled. "My brother let you take José there?

What foolishness. Your old ways aren't our ways anymore. They're just superstitions."

"You think you are wise, but you are foolish. The spirits don't have to prove they're real. They are, that is all, whether you believe in them or not." Tomas kicked his mule into a trot, leaving José with his uncle.

Uncle Miguel laughed. "Well, did you see anything at that rock, eh? Did you see a ghost maybe?"

He tried to ignore his uncle's laughter. José didn't want to tell his uncle about the vision. It was too important to tell someone who would not take it seriously. His uncle would only laugh if he said he had seen Santo in a vision, and that the horse had spoken to him.

Instead of answering, José asked, "What news do you have?"

"I will tell you when you get home. I'm on my way to see your papa. I'll let him know you are coming." Uncle Miguel's horse kicked up pebbles as he galloped off.

José spurred Amigo into a trot and caught up with Tomas.

"Don't let anyone make you doubt what you saw." Tomas wagged his head and scowled. "Never. Some will try. The spirits have chosen you. Always remember that. It will give you power."

"Don't worry. I won't tell him." José had always looked up to his uncle and was disappointed he couldn't share his vision with him.

"That is wise. We cannot share sacred things with those who do not understand."

It was nearly dark when they reached the rancho, and the smell of bread baking in the *horno* lingered around the barnyard. Before going into the adobe, he helped Tomas unsaddle the mule and turned his horse out to pasture.

"*Gracias*, Tomas, for taking me to the painted rock. I'll never forget."

Inside his family's small *casa*, he found his uncle, papa and brothers talking and eating.

"You've returned," his papa greeted him. "I hope your journey was a good one."

"*Sí*, Papa." He spooned simmering stew into a plate and sat to listen.

"Your uncle is telling us about his adventures with Fremont. Have you returned a rich man, Miguel?"

"No, no money, only a promise. I don't think I'll see the twenty-five dollars." Miguel shook his head. "They say Alta California now belongs to the United States, and we are Americans now."

"Americans? How are they different from Mexicans?" José asked.

"For one thing, they don't speak Spanish," Uncle Miguel said. "They speak English. Captain Truckee has guided many American settlers coming west in wagons over the mountains. Now he says more will come."

"Will the Americans make us move from the rancho like we had to move from the mission when Mexico claimed California?" Diego asked.

José began to worry. How would his life change because of the new government? Would he have to learn English? He was a vaquero. Wouldn't the Americans need vaqueros to herd the thousands of cattle that roamed the vast land?

"The ranchero was an American before he became a Mexican," Uncle Miguel said. "He'll know how to deal with this new government and read the many papers they are always signing. *Sí*, he will know."

"Do Americans love gold?" José asked.

Diego nodded. "Gold? Most men love gold. It drives some men loco. They do crazy things to get it. Why do you think of gold?"

José furrowed his brow. "Do you think there is gold in the mountains?"

"It is there," Uncle Miguel said. "Gold can make a man rich. But it isn't easy to find."

"I am already rich." José's papa smiled at him.

Chest swelled with gladness, José lowered his eyes so no one would notice his pride. His papa was the finest vaquero on the rancho. All he had to give his sons was his knowledge and skill with horses and cattle. He was proud of his family, and José didn't want to disappoint him.

The next morning, inside the blacksmith's shed, the beautiful silver bit Pedro made for Santo lay on the workbench. Even in the dull light, the silver gleamed. José picked up the bit and fingered the fine silver.

"You like it, eh?" Pedro asked.

In the dim shed, José had not seen Pedro, and surprised, jumped at his voice.

Pedro laughed. "Santo will like wearing such a fine bit. He will say *gracias*, Señor Pedro, when his tongue slides over the copper roller."

José nodded and laid the bit on the workbench and wondered what Pedro would say if he knew Santo had spoken. Should he tell him about his vision? Perhaps, like Uncle Miguel, he would think it was silly.

"I was looking for you yesterday," Pedro said. "I heard you went to the mountains."

"I returned last night."

"I have something for you." Pedro reached under his workbench and pulled out a pair of sharp-roweled spurs. "Here, try these on." Pedro chuckled and handed the spurs to José.

He smiled. "Oh, have you finished my new spurs?" He sat to slip them on the heels of his boots, noticed a glimmer, and peered at the spurs more closely. On the spur's shank, the letters JR were etched in silver. José looked up. "What is this, Pedro?"

"You said you wanted a pair of silver spurs? When I made Santo's bit, I saved a little silver. I don't think Santo will miss it. I marked your spurs with your brand. Now everyone will know they are yours. Eh?"

A wide grin spread across José's face. "These are the most beautiful spurs I have ever seen. *Gracias.*" He didn't know what else to say.

Silver spurs were just what he'd wanted. Even better, they were marked with his brand, a shiny JR. He traced his finger over his silver initials. He couldn't read or write, but he knew brands.

He slipped the spurs on his heels, and the huge rowels grated and jangled as he strutted around the blacksmith's shop.

Pedro grinned. "You sound like the greatest vaquero in Alta California."

"I can hardly wait to use them." José was sure these spurs were lucky.

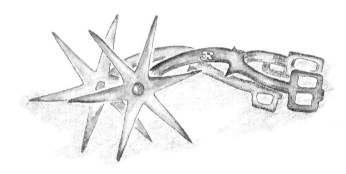

Chapter Twelve
~ Bravo~

It was the day. José had to muster his courage and prove himself worthy of being a vaquero. This morning, he would ride with his brothers to help his papa train the wild colts. Last night, he had lain awake praying for rain, hoping to put off this dreaded day.

With trembling hands, he wrapped his lucky bull hide chaps around his thighs. On his heels, the new spurs clanked loudly. Wearing his lucky spurs and chaps, José thought he would feel brave.

He was wrong.

As he tightened the cinch on Amigo's saddle, a knot of fear squeezed his chest. He wanted to mount his horse and gallop away. But where could he go? Maybe north to work on another rancho, except it would be cowardly to run away. He would be disgraced and disappoint Papa.

"Let's go," Diego told his sons. "We'll push the horses into the boxed canyon, the *corral de piedra*." He spun his horse and galloped toward the grasslands, now green with lush spring grass.

José sucked in a deep breath and mounted Amigo. He and his brothers chased behind their papa until the horse herd came into sight. "José ride next to me," Diego yelled. "We'll circle the horses and rope the bell mare."

He quickly joined his papa. His brother roped the old, white mare, and the colts followed her up the valley and into the wide mouth of the boxed canyon.

Diego slowed his horse. "Ride easy now. We'll drive them into the canyon and trap them."

José's brother turned the bell mare loose to join and quiet the herd, and they pushed the wild horses deeper into the canyon.

The sides of the canyon narrowed until the almost vertical walls were only ten feet apart. José's papa pointed toward a gate almost hidden behind a bush. "José, get off your horse and drag that gate across the trail and block it."

Leading José's horse, his brothers and papa rode farther up the trail and waited while he struggled to place the gate across the trail to block the narrow opening. When he mounted Amigo again, everyone positioned their horses in front of the barrier.

Soon the horse herd rushed back out of the canyon at a brisk trot. Startled by the waiting horsemen, the wild colts stopped and stared, ears alert. Then the suspicious herd spun and galloped deeper into the canyon.

Now, they followed the horses to the canyon's dead-end where the narrow walls widened into a large natural rock corral. Here the high-headed mustangs huddled together.

"Look them over, and pick your colts," Diego instructed his sons. "The ones you choose will be yours to train. Only you will ride them. José, you get the first choice."

José rode closer to the herd. The wild horses' fear matched his own. His stomach quivered like a tarantula's spidery legs crawled around inside. He tried not to think about it. Fear must not control him. He must choose his colts.

He knew what to look for in a good horse, well-shaped withers to hold the saddle, legs straight and strong, a head not too large, or eyes too small. Earlier he had spotted a palomino colt and without thinking of the perfect head, or legs, or eyes, he said, "The golden one. I choose the golden stallion."

His papa laughed and nodded. "The golden one. He is the envy of all the other ranchos. When you ride him, everyone will notice. Lasso him, José."

José's hands trembled. His brothers and papa were watching. He wanted to impress them with a clean catch on his first throw. The horses were already familiar with the lasso.

After their mamas had weaned them, his papa had lassoed these colts and tied them to a bell mare. She became their new mama, and they learned to respect the reata and follow her.

Now, the quiet bell mare kept the colts together, making it easier to catch them. José slowly rode into the herd, trying not to frighten the young horses. If the colts panicked and ran, catching one would be more difficult.

The golden horse was aware of José's every movement. He approached the palomino, then stopped and waited, taking his time. Amigo was patient, too.

The golden colt stood, watching José and Amigo. Curious about the strange horse, it wasn't long before he overcame his distrust, nosed Amigo, and squealed.

José's drumming heartbeat slowed to an even thump as he eased Amigo alongside the palomino. He felt the young stallion's warm breath as he slipped a noose over the colt's head and tied the reata to the saddle horn.

The horse didn't panic until the loop tightened around his throat. Surprised and frightened, the colt began struggling, rearing, and fighting the lasso.

"Easy, easy," José's papa warned. "Follow him, don't fight him. Little by little, pull and follow, until he quiets and remembers the feel of the lasso and the lesson the bell mare taught him."

Sweat beaded on José's face as he rode Amigo close beside the young horse, walking forward and following when the colt pulled back.

Many minutes passed before the colt snorted and stopped pulling, panting and rolling his eyes in fear. José knew the colt's fear and felt sorry for him. He carefully reached out and stroked the stallion's flowing blond mane and the sweaty crest of his neck.

At the first touch, the colt rolled his eyes and looked back at him. Then gradually, the horse stopped trembling. José sighed and felt calmer, too.

"He is beginning to trust you," Papa said. "Try leading him now. See if he remembers."

"Come with me, and we will go many places together," José whispered, held his breath and gently tugged on the reata.

The colt no longer pulled back and took one step. Then step by step, the young horse began to follow Amigo around the rocky corral.

Diego rode up next to Amigo. "José, tie your horse to a hitching post and catch another one."

Near the corral's rocky walls, four hitching posts were anchored in the ground. He led the colt to a tie post and dismounted. Not used to seeing a man on foot, once again, the young horse shied and tried to pull away. José stepped back, hid behind Amigo, and managed to tie the colt securely to a post.

He quietly slipped around Amigo. When the colt saw him so near, he pulled back again. "You'll get used to me," José whispered, and leaving the colt snubbed to the post, mounted Amigo.

While José had been leading his golden colt, his brothers chose the horses they would train. Though still tense when he rode back into the herd to catch another horse, he felt more confident. The lucky chaps and spurs *were* protecting him. He spent the day catching, tying, and then releasing the colts.

That evening, the horses were driven out of the box canyon. "Tomorrow, they will have the same lesson until they are ready to be ridden," Diego said. "It is wise to go slowly and be on your guard when training these wild colts. We won't rush them. With slow and easy training, they will learn to trust us and become able and brave cow horses."

After a week of catching and gentling the horses, like the colts, José's fear dwindled. Dew still wet the grass as he rode out in the early morning with his papa and brothers. The small herd grazed near the opening of *corral de piedra*.

"*Gracias, caballos*," José said. "You make it easy for us to catch you today." Again capturing the horses in the canyon, he lassoed the golden palomino. The colt no longer snorted or rolled his eyes in panic while led around the corral.

Diego nodded. "Today, maybe he will wear the saddle. Tie him, sack him out. Rub your serape all over his body. Then, if he's ready, saddle him. Take your time. There is no hurry."

José's stomach tightened. He hoped the colt was ready. As he led him to the hitching post, the palomino became alert. When he dismounted, the clank of José's lucky spurs gave him confidence. He shrugged his shoulders and began to relax.

Sensing the horse's fear and distrust, he stroked the colt's neck. After a few minutes, the palomino seemed to relax, too. Using his serape, he warily began to rub it over the horse's back and legs.

Surprised and frightened, the young horse kicked and stomped. Ready for the colt to resist, José quickly jumped out of the way of the dangerous hooves.

With quaky knees, he took a deep breath and again tried to rub the serape over the horse's back. Again, the colt defended against the strange thing touching him by kicking and pulling back.

"Don't be afraid," José whispered. "Be a brave stallion like Santo. Then I will name you *Oro Bravo*."

Again and again, he sacked out the colt, and, after much patience and effort, the palomino finally stood quietly when the serape was laid on his back.

"*Bueno*," Diego said. "It is time for the saddle."

"Easy, easy, Bravo." José carefully hoisted the saddle onto his back.

Bravo did not fight until the saddle was cinched. Then he snorted and struggled against the tie rope, lunging and rearing as the lasso tightened around his neck.

José leaped out of the way and watched while the palomino decided whether to accept the scary thing strapped on his back.

"When he quits arguing with that saddle," Diego instructed, "lead him around."

Bravo finally calmed. José mounted Amigo, untied the palomino, and led him around the box canyon. When the saddle squeaked and shifted on his back, Bravo became frightened again and lunged, bucked and kicked. As Amigo pulled against the golden colt, the reata tightened around the saddle horn. Finally, Bravo settled down. With only occasional stomps and hops, he followed Amigo.

Diego had been watching his son gentle the colt. "He is ready to be unsaddled."

The rest of the day, José's hands barely trembled when he saddled his other colts. After all the horses had been handled, they were again turned out to pasture.

On the ride home, his papa noticed José wore spurs. "Your new spurs are beautiful, José, but no spurs tomorrow. Tomorrow, we will ride our colts, and these young horses are not yet ready for the prick of a spur."

It was strange. While taming the colts, his hands had trembled and his heart had raced, but fear had not stopped him. Instead, it made him more aware, ready for what the colts might do next. But tomorrow, when he rode the wild ones, it might not be the same.

That night, he barely closed his eyes in sleep. He got up and threw a log into the fire. Wrapping his serape around his shoulders, he sat near the warmth of the flames and considered.

Maybe he should go. Without his lucky spurs, he might not be able to stay on the colts if they bucked and reared. He could end up like Tomas, crippled for life. If he was going to leave, now was the time. In the middle of the night, before his family awoke.

Staring into the flames, he shook his head. No, he could not leave. To slink away in fear would be shameful. Without courage, he would never be a man. He would never be a vaquero.

The next morning, José's queasy stomach twisted in a knot as he tied on the bull hide chaps. Maybe wearing the chaps would be enough to bring him the luck he needed. All he could do was hope. For good luck's sake, he firmly tied his spurs onto his saddle.

José helped drive the colts into the rocky canyon. With a wave of his hand, his papa signaled him. "Lasso your golden colt. You'll ride first."

His brothers and papa watched while he lassoed and saddled Bravo. Today, the stallion didn't buck or fight.

After the colt was saddled, instead of José, his papa untied him and led him around the corral. Diego shortened the lead rope, snugged it tightly to his saddle horn, and pulled Bravo's head close to his horse's shoulder.

Now, prepared for anything the colt might do he said, "It is time. He is ready now, José."

José's knees wobbled like willow twigs. He told himself to be brave, but no matter how hard he tried, he couldn't make his hands or knees stop trembling.

"Easy, José. Stand in the stirrup awhile." Diego held the colt's head high and waited for his son to step into the stirrup. "Let him feel your weight and know it is you above him. It is good to be cautious. Caution is what keeps a vaquero alive."

José's chaps felt heavy as he gripped the hackamore's prickly horsehair reins and hoisted himself up into the stirrup.

"Don't hurry."

His papa's voice soothed José's fear. His knee quit shaking and his leg grew tired standing and waiting with one foot in the stirrup.

When Bravo stood calmly, Diego whispered, "Ease your leg over slowly. Quiet and easy. Don't surprise him. It's better if he never learns to buck."

José tried to swallow, but his mouth was too dry. Holding his breath, he eased his right leg over Bravo's back and into the stirrup.

The palomino snorted when he felt José's weight settle into the saddle. Diego held the horse and calmed him, and then led José and Bravo around the rock corral.

When the colt seemed quiet, Diego said, "Now, you are on your own," and released the colt.

Bravo stood frozen.

José turned the colt's nose with the hackamore reins, trying to get him to move forward. Since the colt no longer had another horse to lean against, he stepped in the direction his nose had been turned.

With the strange weight on his back, the palomino wavered and wobbled. Surprised by the horse's unsure steps, José steadied his seat to keep his balance. This made Bravo jump forward, bucking and kicking his hind feet high in the air. It happened so fast José had no time to worry about being brave or looking foolish.

"Lean back and ride him," his brother yelled.

Bravo bucked and lunged. Still holding the reins, José struggled to pull the colt's head up to stop him.

Bravo took a huge leap, and a front leg reached so high it tangled in the hackamore's reins. As Bravo tumbled toward the ground, José quickly kicked his feet out of the stirrups and rolled off and out of the way of scrambling hooves.

Stunned, José lay in the dirt, staring at the sky. His confused brain cleared, and he turned his head to look over at the colt.

A few feet away, the palomino lay motionless.

José rolled over onto his knees, crawled to the golden horse, and stroked his thick crest. "Bravo.

Bravo. Wake up."

Chapter Thirteen
~ Amigos~

He peered into Bravo's glazed eye. No light flickered in the stallion's dark pupil. "Don't die, Bravo," José moaned. "Don't give up."

Bravo continued lying stretched on the ground. José said a prayer as he rubbed the colt's ears. But the horse still lay as if in a trance. Only his ribs heaved up and down with each heavy breath.

José laid his hand over Bravo's soft nostril and felt hot breath against his fingers. Then the colt heaved a great sigh, twitched his ears, and lifted his head.

José wanted to shout with happiness but knew it might frighten the colt. Instead, he whispered, "Lie still, Bravo. Get your wind. You'll be all right."

"Give him time to recover," Diego said. "After that fall, he needs a little rest."

After a few minutes of stroking Bravo's neck, José untangled the reins from the colt's legs and tugged on them to encourage him to stand. "Please get up, Bravo. You need to get up. You cannot rest all day."

The colt lifted his head, looked around, then stretched his forelegs out and with a tremendous grunt, awkwardly jerked his heavy body off the ground. Once on his feet, he lowered his head and shook from head to tail, sending dust flying and rattling the saddle.

Relieved the noise of the shaking saddle didn't scare the colt, José checked him for injury and then led him around the corral. He showed no signs of a limp.

José whispered a prayer of thanks and made the sign of the cross. Then he gathered the reins, pulled the colt's head to one side, carefully stepped up, and stood in the stirrup.

Taking a deep breath, he slowly placed his leg over the colt's back. Ready for another upset, he carefully settled into the saddle. But Bravo stood as nicely as Amigo did when mounted.

"*Muy Bueno.* You are *bravo.*" José sat quietly in the saddle, stroking the colt's neck. At least five minutes passed before he gently turned the horse's nose to urge him forward. The wobbly-legged colt took a step, then two, then three, and slowly got his balance as he walked around the corral.

"Good work," his papa said.

"The golden colt is *muy bravo.*" José smiled for he had ridden well. Maybe he was a little bit brave, too. Even though afraid, he had mounted the colt after the terrible fall. Like his papa said, fear kept him alert and ready. Once mounted, his attention turned to training the colt like a real vaquero.

"Ride around the corral once more, then unsaddle and catch another colt. The day is short. We have many other colts to start." His papa and brothers rode into the herd and each caught a horse to ride.

José dismounted, unsaddled, and stroked Bravo's muscular neck and shoulders. The palomino no longer trembled at his touch. He gazed into the colt's eyes and no longer saw fear. "Bravo, today we have become *amigos.*"

He released Bravo from the tie post, then mounted his horse and rode back into the herd and lassoed another colt. The day was a long one.

José and his brothers saddled and rode many horses. Some bucked wildly, snorting and twisting. After the day was over, even though he was worried and nervous before mounting each young horse, it did not matter. He had swallowed his fear and rode them.

After the colts had been driven out of the rock corral, his papa halted his horse next to José. Diego took off his hat, wiped his brow, and looked at his son. "The colts responded well to your hand. Hands of a true vaquero talk to his horse."

He paused to shorten his reins. "You have such hands. Not every man can think like a horse, read his mind and know what he will do before he does it. It is a gift. I think you have this gift. Today was a good day."

On the way home, José rode beside his papa. He tucked his chin against his chest, watched his horse's ears, and tried to hide his pride. Many times, he had heard a vaquero was only as good as the horse he rode. He must remember, a good *caballo* made a good vaquero, not the other way around. His papa had carefully chosen the string of good colts they were training as cow horses. Except, Bravo was better than good. He was excellent.

Even so, his papa had said José had a gift. "Papa, is a gift the same as being lucky?"

Diego laughed. "Having a gift is very lucky."

Chapter Fourteen
~ *Gold Fever*~

José kept busy riding his string of horses. He had to train them to rope calves for the next rodeo where during the excitement of branding, anything might happen. Bravo was his favorite. The golden palomino stallion's summer coat glistened. When he rode him around the rancho, envious eyes followed them.

One afternoon, Pedro rode up and watched José circling Bravo in the pasture, teaching him to stop and turn quickly as a cow horse must. He slid Bravo to a stop in front of Pedro's horse, tipped his hat and grinned. "Have you come to see if your spurs have worked their magic and made me the greatest vaquero in Alta California?"

Pedro slapped his knee and laughed. "I come to see you ride because Bravo is beautiful. I like watching him. He is a great horse. If I were a vaquero, I would ride a fine horse like Bravo."

Pedro swatted a horsefly that landed on his mare's neck. "I wish I could ride as well as you. I've been practicing roping and am getting pretty good. But my mare doesn't know how to hold a calf, and I don't know how to train her. Will you help me?"

José looked down at the spurs on his heels with JR branded in silver that Pedro had made. The gift made it hard to say no. "I will help you. Show me what you can do with that reata tied to your saddle."

Pedro gathered his lasso and shook out a loop. Twirling it overhead, he threw it and caught a nearby bush. "I can catch any bush I want, but this horse wouldn't like it if I caught a wild calf."

"Tomorrow, I will let you ride Amigo. He will teach you to

be a vaquero." Bravo snorted and fussed at Pedro's mare as they jogged side-by-side back to the rancho.

The next day, they found a few cows and calves wandering together in the valley. While José trained a young colt, Pedro practiced roping from Amigo. José stopped his horse and watched while he roped his first calf. Pedro whooped with excitement when he caught the calf on his first try. He patted Amigo's neck and kept the reata taut as the calf jumped and kicked, trying to escape.

"*Bueno*, Pedro, maybe you will become a vaquero."

"If I keep practicing and getting better, maybe I can help at the rodeo." Pedro stared at José. "Will you ask your papa?"

"If Papa will let you ride Amigo, maybe you can try your skills at the rodeo." José pushed his hat back to wipe his brow. "I will ask. But the rodeo is fast and dangerous. You must understand the cattle are mean and wild and get angry if you don't know how to handle them. Bad things happen fast. If they do, you must be ready."

José picked up his reins and smiled. "Work the cattle and you'll learn. Now that you've caught that calf, how are you going to release him?" After showing Pedro how to flip the loop off the calf's neck, he continued training his colt.

Every day, Pedro practiced, working hard to learn how to rope calves and hold them tightly with the reata. The day before the next rodeo, Pedro was ready. When José went to the blacksmith's shop to get a bit left there for repair, Pedro asked, "Did you find out if I could ride Amigo and help at the rodeo?"

"*Sí*. You can help gather the herd. Papa said he'd see how well you handle the cattle, then decide if you're good enough to rope."

"*Gracias*." Pleased to be able to help at the rodeo, Pedro lowered his chin to hide a smile. He gave the iron bit he'd fixed one last inspection before returning it to José.

The next morning, the vaqueros were up early to round up the cattle that roamed Rancho Grande's thirty-eight-thousand acres. José and Pedro's horses trotted up steep mountains to find the wild cows. Bravo and Amigo almost sat on their rumps while sliding on their hocks down deep arroyos.

They looked for cows in canyons and galloped along rocky slopes, pushing cattle into the valley. The clever cattle hid in the brush, silently waiting for the riders to pass by. The vaqueros searched through the brush and tall mustard, stampeding the balky cows and calves out of their hiding places.

It was late in the day before all the cattle were gathered. That evening, the vaqueros made camp near the clustered herd. During the night, they took turns keeping the cows together, ready for tomorrow's branding. The vaqueros sat by the campfire listening to each other's stories when someone yelled, *"Buenas noches."*

José rose from his place at the fire to see who had ridden into camp and shouted, "It's Uncle Miguel."

Diego stood and greeted his brother. "What brings you?"

"I delivered horses to the rancho on the other side of the pass and heard some news. They've found gold in the mountains. Everyone is leaving to search for it. I'm going, too. It's my chance to make a fortune. You should come. I heard nuggets were everywhere. Easy pickings. Soon everyone will hear the news. If we go now, we can get there first."

Many of the vaqueros agreed and were impatient to leave. "Let's go. We'll be rich," was repeated around the camp. The possibility of finding gold so easily had stirred them up.

It worried Diego the men were so eager to leave. "Wait, we cannot just go. There is a herd of calves to brand. Besides, how do we know this is true? Where did you hear this, Miguel?"

"Someone read it in a San Francisco newspaper." Miguel's voice grew louder and more excited telling about the riches just waiting to be plucked off the ground. "If it was in the newspaper, it must be true. The mountains are full of gold. There is enough for everyone."

As José listened, Santo's warning echoed in his mind. Now

he knew the meaning of his vision. Searching in the mountains for gold would bring death. José knew his uncle probably would not believe in his vision, but he must be warned.

"Uncle Miguel, it could be dangerous looking for gold in the mountains," he said, hoping his uncle would listen.

"Could it be any more dangerous than the work we do?" Miguel asked. "Vaqueros face danger every day. These wild cows are loco. Finding gold and getting rich would be worth the risk."

"*Sí, sí,*" some of the vaqueros said. "Let's go tomorrow."

No one would listen. José knew it was hopeless. The only vision Uncle Miguel believed in was his dream of piles of gold. He wouldn't change his mind about going into the mountains to find his fortune.

As many of the vaqueros made plans to leave, Diego said, "Wait. I'll go get the ranchero." He leaped from his horse and hurried to the ranchero's *casa*.

All the talk of gold stirred up Pedro's hopes. "I could find enough gold to buy a little rancho."

José wanted to warn Pedro too. Afraid he wouldn't listen, he grasped his shoulder. "I must tell you about my dream. Don't laugh. It is too important."

"I won't laugh. We should listen to our dreams. I've known people whose dreams have come true. What did your dream tell you?"

"Do you remember when we found the painted cave?" José asked. "Tomas thought the spirits led us there, and they wanted to tell me something."

He watched to see if Pedro smiled. When he didn't, he continued. "That is why I went to the sacred rock. I had a dream there. I didn't know what it meant until now."

José waited, still not sure if he should tell about the vision.

Pedro grew impatient. "Well, tell me."

"It was Santo. He came to me in a vision." José peered into

Pedro's eyes. "He said, 'Don't look for gold in the mountains. Death waits there.' When I asked what he meant, he said, 'You will know when you know.' Until now, I didn't understand. We must not go into the mountains and look for gold. We should stay here on the rancho."

Pedro squinted his eyes as he gazed at José. "It was your vision, not mine. Maybe the message was only meant as a warning for you."

José nodded. "Perhaps. That is possible. But you were with me in the cave the night of the storm. Maybe it was also a message for you. After all, the spirits led you to the painted cave too."

Pedro shrugged. "Gold would make me rich. I could be a ranchero. I could marry Carmelita and give her beautiful things."

"If Carmelita loves you, beautiful things won't matter." José shook his head. "She wouldn't want you to lose your life for riches. The spirits do not lie. I'm not going into those mountains. I am a vaquero. My life is here. If you want to be a vaquero, your life is here, too."

"I will think about it," was all Pedro would promise.

Chapter Fifteen
~ *Adios*~

After that night, things changed on the rancho. Even though the ranchero promised the vaqueros higher wages, many left to seek gold in the mountains.

"I cannot afford to lose you. If you stay, I will give you a herd of horses," the ranchero promised Diego. "You will have higher wages and your horses to sell."

Rancho Grande bred the finest horses in California, and many rancheros came to buy them. Diego and his sons agreed to stay.

"Papa, will you choose Bravo?" José asked. "He is smart, very fast, and has become a fine cow horse. He will be a great sire of many golden foals."

"He would make a great sire. I'll include him with the horses I choose. Since you have done such a fine job training him, he will be yours."

The blacksmith, Eduardo Garcia, was also promised increased wages and decided to stay on the rancho. Pedro stayed and worked with his papa, earning not only blacksmith wages, but also vaquero wages. Often, José and Pedro earned money helping at other ranchos because many of their workers had left for the goldfields.

Many evenings, José visited the warmth of the blacksmith's shed. In the dim light of the forge's glowing coals, he sat on a stool and listened to Pedro make plans for his money. "With all this work and the extra wages, I'll soon have enough money to marry Carmelita."

Pedro included José in his plans. "You and I should go in together and use our money to buy a rancho. We could own many cattle and horses. The gold miners are hungry. The cattle prices are high in San Francisco. We could be rich."

"Perhaps."

One morning, Tomas peered into the blacksmith's shed. "Are you in here, José?"

"I am."

"I want to say *adios*."

"What? Are you leaving? Where are you going?"

"To be with my mama's people." Tomas wiped his eyes with his work stained fingers. "I must travel to the sacred rock once more. My people will be gathered there, and I will join them. When my time comes, they will bury me."

"Tomas, you cannot leave. Your home is here."

"No, José. When I was born at the mission, Spain owned Alta California. I was still young when Mexico took the church's land, and I had to find a new home on the rancho. I've seen two countries claim California, and now another will possess her. There will be more changes. I am too old and tired to change. It is time for me to go."

Though over a year since his visit to the sacred rock, José would never forget that trip or his vision. He worried the old man couldn't make a trip that far alone. "I'll travel to the sacred rock with you."

"No. I must make this journey without you. You and Pedro are young. Your future is here. You are vaqueros. Never forget to be proud of who you are. I just wanted to say *adios*." Tomas turned to leave.

"Wait, at least let me ride with you to the top of the mountains." José couldn't believe Tomas was leaving. He had always lived on the rancho. Perhaps on the way, he could change Tomas's mind.

"Follow if you must, just to the mountain top, but no farther." Tomas mounted his mule and rode off.

José quickly saddled Bravo. Pedro joined him and saddled Amigo. They jumped on their horses and in a gallop, caught up with Tomas's mule. Together, they quietly rode toward the steep mountains that blocked entry into the inland valley.

Climbing the mountain was the most difficult part of the journey. Only shuffled hoof steps broke the silence as they climbed the mountain's rocky, zigzag trail. Tomas never stopped to rest his mule or look back until he reached the top.

There, he halted. "*Adios*, José. *Adios*, Pedro. Now you must return to the rancho."

Tomas gazed at the sky and waited for the boys to turn back.

José's chest tightened as he fought back his tears. Tomas was his friend. It didn't seem right leaving an old half-blind man to wander into the hills alone. "Are you sure we cannot go with you, Tomas?"

Tomas tightened his lips into a grimace. He said nothing, just waited.

Pedro reached over and squeezed José's arm. "Come. We must go."

The old man sat on his mule in stubborn silence. He lowered his pale, watery eyes and stared at his hands with an empty gaze. Tomas would never change his mind.

José sighed. "*Vaya con Dios*, Tomas. I will miss you." He sadly turned Bravo toward home. As he rode away, he twisted in the saddle to wave a final goodbye.

Tomas was gone.

Only once did José and Pedro stop to rest the horses on the steep descent back to the coastal valley. Below them the brilliant sunshine shimmered off the blue-green ocean, and the white dunes stretched for miles and miles along the coast of the new California.

Story Questions

Who were the vaqueros?

Why was their job important?

Where did Tomas learn to be a vaquero?

Why did Tomas leave the mission to work on the rancho?

What was the main industry in Alta California in 1846?

What language did José speak on the Alta California rancho?

What was daily life like on a rancho?

What reason might the ranchero who owned Rancho Grande help Colonel Fremont?

How did life on the rancho change when gold was discovered in California?

Design A Brand

Materials needed- paper and pencil.

The main industry of California's rancho period was the hide and tallow trade. The valuable cowhides were called "California Banknotes."

With hundreds of ranchos and no fences, thousands of cattle roamed freely. A brand was needed to determine ownership.

Today, we brand cattle to establish ownership and register the brand just as they did during the days of the ranchos.

Imagine you own a huge ranch like Rancho Grande. Name your ranch and design a brand by using letters or numbers, or a combination of the two. Perhaps use your initials. A simple, easy-to-read design is best. After drawing the brand, share your ranch's name and why you chose the design of your brand.

Porter Ranch Brand

Words to Know

adios: good-by
amigo: friend
arroyo: gully
bravo: brave
buenos días: good day
buenas noches: good night
caballo: horse
casa: home
corral de piedra: rock enclosure
frijoles: beans
gracias: thank you
hackamore: a halter with reins used to train horses
jerky: thin strips of salted meat sun-dried or smoked to preserve it
La Noche Buena: Christmas Eve
oro: gold
palomino: a horse with a golden color and a blond mane and tail
reata: a rope made of braided rawhide
rodeo: gathering cattle for branding
sí: yes
santo: saint
vaya con Dios: God be with you
vaquero: cowboy

Bibliography

ANGEL, MYRON. *History of San Luis Obispo County California 1883.* Friends of the Adobes, 1994.

BENEFIELD, HATTIE STONE. *For the Good of the Country.* Privately Published, 1951.

BRYANT, EDWIN. *What I Saw in California.* University of Nebraska Press, 1985.

BROWN, VINSON. *Voices of Earth and Sky.* Naturegraph Publishers, 1976.

DANA, RICHARD HENRY, JR. *Two Years Before the Mast.* The Modern Library, 2001.

DANA, ROCKY & HARRINGTON, MARIE. *The Blond Ranchero.* South County Historical Society, Second Edition 1999.

DARY, DAVID. *Cowboy Culture A Saga of Five Centuries.* University Press of Kansas, 1989.

ENGELHARDT, ZEPHYRIN. *Mission San Luis Obispo in the Valley of the Bears.* Imprint Santa Barbara California; W.T. Genns, 1963.

GRANT, BRUCE. *How to Make Cowboy Horse Gear.* Cornell Maritime Press, 1956.

HEIZER ROBERT F. & ELSASSER ALBERT B. *The Natural World of the California Indians.* University of California Press, 1980.

KROEBER, A.L. *Handbook of California Indians.* Washington D.C., 1925.

LIBRADO, FERNANDO. *Breath of the Sun: life in early California/ as told by a Chumash Indian, Fernando Librado, to John P. Harrington: Edited with notes by Travis, H.* Malki Museum Press, 1980.

MONROY, DOUGLAS. *Thrown Among Strangers.* The University of California Press, 1993.

MORA, JO. *Californios: the Saga of the Hard-Riding Vaqueros, America's First Cowboys.* Doubleday, 1949.

ROBINSON, ALFRED. *Life in California.* Da Capo Press, 1969.

SMEAD, ROBERT N. *Vocabulario Vaquero/Cowboy Talk: A Dictionary of Spanish Terms from the American West.* University of Oklahoma Press, 2004.

STORER, TRACY I. & TEVIS, LLOYD P. *California Grizzly.* University of Nebraska Press, 1978.

TRAFZER, CLIFFORD E. *American Indians as Cowboys.* Sierra Oaks Publishing Company, 1992.

California Indians and the Gold Rush. Sierra Oaks Publishing Company, 1989.

Captain Portola in San Luis Obispo County in 1769: Portions of the Diary of Fr. Juan Crespi, O.F.M: as edited and augmented from other diaries by his colleague Fr. Francisco Palou. Tabula Rasa Press, 1984.

California's Chumash Indians. Santa Barbara Museum of Natural History, 1986.

About the Author

Wanda Snow Porter lives in Nipomo, a small town on the central coast of California. An avid horsewoman, she learned the vaquero way of training horses, earned the United States Dressage Federation's Bronze Medal Rider's Award, and taught horseback riding.

Her knowledge of horses, history, and art inspires her to illustrate and write stories for children and adults.

http://www.WandaSnowPorter.com

Other Books by Wanda Snow Porter

Novels

Remedy
Riding Babyface
Ordinary Miracles

Non-fiction

Voyages of No Return:
Mutiny on the HMS Bounty and Beyond

Picture Books

Sister Sara the Adobe Burro
Blanco
Emily Decides
Capturing Time
Christmas Kitten
Horses Change Coats

Made in United States
Orlando, FL
20 May 2022

18036271R00059